DOVER · THRIFT · EDITIONS

The Overcoat
and Other Short Stories

NIKOLAI GOGOL

DOVER PUBLICATIONS, INC.
New York

DOVER THRIFT EDITIONS

EDITOR: STANLEY APPELBAUM

This Dover edition, first published in 1992, is an unabridged republication of four stories.
"The Nose" is reprinted, by permission of Mary Struve, from *Russian Stories / Russkie
Rasskazy: A Dual-Language Book*, edited by Gleb Struve, Dover Publications, Inc., 1990
(original edition: Bantam Books, Inc., N.Y., 1961); the translation is by Gleb and Mary Struve.
"Old-Fashioned Farmers," "The Tale of How Ivan Ivanovich Quarrelled with Ivan
Nikiforovich" and "The Overcoat" are reprinted from *St. John's Eve and Other Stories*, Thomas
Y. Crowell & Co., N.Y., 1886; the translations are by Isabel F. Hapgood; "The Overcoat"
appears there as "The Cloak." Wording, spelling, punctuation and paragraphing of the Hapgood text have been freely altered for the present edition, and additional footnotes and bracketed
explanations of Russian terms have been newly added. The Note was written specially for the
Dover edition.

Manufactured in the United States of America
Dover Publications, Inc., 31 East 2nd Street, Mineola, N.Y. 11501

Library of Congress Cataloging-in-Publication Data

Gogol', Nikolaĭ Vasil'evich, 1809–1852.
   [Short stories. English. Selections]
   The overcoat and other short stories / Nikolai Gogol. — Dover Thrift ed.
     p.   cm.
   Translated from the Russian.
   ISBN 0-486-27057-2
   1. Gogol', Nikolaĭ Vasil'evich, 1809–1852—Translations into English. I. Title.
PG3333.A6   1992
891.73'3—dc20
                                                            91-34212
                                                              CIP

Note

THE RUSSIAN WRITER NIKOLAI GOGOL (1809–1852) is admired for his novel *Dead Souls* and his play *The Inspector General* as well as for a number of outstanding short stories. Of the four representative stories chosen for this volume, "Old-Fashioned Farmers" (also known as "Old-World Landowners") and "The Tale of How Ivan Ivanovich Quarrelled with Ivan Nikiforovich"—both of which originally appeared in the collection *Mirgorod* in 1835—depict small-town life in the author's native Ukraine. "The Nose"—originally published in 1836 in Pushkin's magazine *Sovremennik* (The Contemporary)—and "The Overcoat" (also known as "The Cloak")—originally published in the third volume of Gogol's collected works in 1842—reflect the bureaucratic life in the Tsarist capital, St. Petersburg.

The unifying factors in all four stories are the author's amazing powers of observation, his nervous prose style and his gift for social satire. This satire is gentle and loving in "Old-Fashioned Farmers," becomes truly burlesque (but with a melancholy aftertaste) in the tale of the two Ivans, mingles with sheer fantasy in "The Nose" and is heavily tinged with moralistic bitterness in "The Overcoat." Gogol's stories exerted a decided influence on such later Russian authors as Dostoyevsky, and have continued to inspire writers in many other parts of the world.

Contents

Old-Fashioned Farmers

I AM VERY FOND of the modest life of those isolated owners of distant villages, which are usually called "old-fashioned" in Little Russia [the Ukraine], and which, like ruinous and picturesque houses, are beautiful through their simplicity and complete contrast to a new, regular building, whose walls the rain has never yet washed, whose roof is not yet covered with mould, and whose porch, undeprived of its stucco, does not yet show its red bricks. I love sometimes to enter for a moment the sphere of this unusually isolated life, where no wish flies beyond the palings surrounding the little yard, beyond the hedge of the garden filled with apples and plums, beyond the izbás [cottages] of the village surrounding it, having on one side, shaded by willows, elder-bushes and pear-trees. The life of the modest owners is so quiet, so quiet, that you forget yourself for a moment, and think that the passions, wishes, and the uneasy offspring of the Evil One, which keep the world in an uproar, do not exist at all, and that you have only beheld them in some brilliant, dazzling vision.

I can see now the low-roofed little house, with its veranda of slender, blackened tree-trunks, surrounding it on all sides, so that, in case of a thunder or hail storm, the window-shutters could be shut without your getting wet; behind it, fragrant wild-cherry trees, whole rows of dwarf fruit-trees, overtopped by crimson cherries and a purple sea of plums, covered with a lead-colored bloom, luxuriant maples, under the shade of which rugs were spread for repose; in front of the house the spacious yard, with short, fresh grass, through which paths had been trodden from the store-houses to the kitchen, from the kitchen to the apartments of the family; a long-legged goose drinking water, with her young goslings, soft as down; the picket-fence hung with bunches of dried pears and apples, and rugs put out to air; a cart full of melons standing near the store-house; the oxen unyoked, and lying lazily beside it.

All this has for me an indescribable charm, perhaps because I no longer see it, and because anything from which we are separated is pleasing to us. However that may be, from the moment that my brichka [trap] drove up to the porch of this little house, my soul entered into a wonderfully pleasant and peaceful state: the horses trotted merrily up to the porch; the coachman climbed very quietly down from the seat, and filled his pipe, as though he had arrived at his own house; the very bark which the phlegmatic dogs set up was soothing to my ears.

But more than all else, the owners of this isolated nook—an old man and old woman—hastening anxiously out to meet me, pleased me. Their faces present themselves to me even now, sometimes, in the crowd and commotion, amid fashionable dress-suits; and then suddenly a half-dreaming state overpowers me, and the past flits before me. On their countenances are always depicted such goodness, such cheerfulness, and purity of heart, that you involuntarily renounce, if only for a brief space of time, all bold conceptions, and imperceptibly enter with all your feelings into this lowly bucolic life.

To this day I cannot forget two old people of the last century, who are, alas! no more; but my heart is still full of pity, and my feelings are strangely moved when I fancy myself driving up sometimes to their former dwelling, now deserted, and see the cluster of decaying cottages, the weedy pond, and, where the little house used to stand, an overgrown pit, and nothing more. It is melancholy. But let us return to our story.

Afanasii Ivanovich Tovstogub, and his wife Pulcheria Ivanovna Tovstogubikha, according to the neighboring muzhiks' [peasants'] way of putting it, were the old people whom I began to tell about. If I were a painter, and wished to represent Philemon and Baucis on canvas, I could have found no better models than they. Afanasii Ivanovich was sixty years old, Pulcheria Ivanovna was fifty-five. Afanasii Ivanovich was tall, always wore a sheepskin jacket covered with camel's hair, sat all doubled up, and was almost always smiling, whether he was telling a story or only listening. Pulcheria Ivanovna was rather serious, and hardly ever laughed; but her face and eyes expressed so much goodness, so much readiness to treat you to all the best they owned, that you would probably have found a smile too repellingly sweet for her kind face.

The delicate wrinkles were so agreeably disposed upon their countenances, that an artist would certainly have appropriated them. It seemed as though you might read their whole life in them, the pure, peaceful life, led by the old patriotic, simple-hearted, and, at the same time, wealthy families, which always offer a contrast to those baser Little Russians, who work up from tar-burners and pedlers, throng the court-rooms like grasshoppers, squeeze the last kopek from their fellow-countrymen, crowd Petersburg with scandal-mongers, finally acquire a capital, and triumphantly add an *f* to their surnames ending in *o*. No, they did not resemble those despicable and miserable creatures, but all ancient and native Little Russian families.

It was impossible to behold without sympathy their mutual affection. They never called each other *thou*, but always *you*—"You, Afanasii Ivanovich"; "You, Pulcheria Ivanovna."

"Was it you who sold the chair, Afanasii Ivanovich?"

"No matter. Don't you be angry, Pulcheria Ivanovna: it was I."

They never had any children, so all their affection was concentrated upon themselves. At one time, in his youth, Afanasii Ivanovich served in the militia, and was afterwards brevet-major; but that was very long ago, and Afanasii Ivanovich hardly ever thought of it himself. Afanasii Ivanovich married at thirty, while he was still young and wore embroidered waist-coats. He even very cleverly abducted Pulcheria Ivanovna, whose parents did not wish to give her to him. But this, too, he recollected very little about; at least, he never mentioned it.

All these long-past and unusual events had given place to a quiet and lonely life, to those dreamy yet harmonious fancies which you experience seated on a country balcony facing the garden, when the beautiful rain patters luxuriously on the leaves, flows in murmuring rivulets, inclining your limbs to repose, and meanwhile the rainbow creeps from behind the trees, and its arch shines dully with its seven hues in the sky; or when your calash rolls on, pushing its way among green bushes, and the quail calls, and the fragrant grass, with the ears of grain and field-flowers, creeps into the door of your carriage, pleasantly striking against your hands and face.

He always listened with a pleasant smile to his guests: sometimes he talked himself, but generally he asked questions. He was not one of the old men who weary you with praises of the old times, and complaints of the new: on the contrary, as he put questions to you, he exhibited the greatest curiosity about, and sympathy with, the circumstances of your life, your success, or lack of success, in which kind old men usually are interested; although it closely resembles the curiosity of a child, who examines the seal on your fob while he is asking his questions. Then, it might be said that his face beamed with kindness.

The rooms of the little house in which our old people lived were small, low-studded, such as are generally to be seen with old-fashioned people. In each room stood a huge stove, which occupied nearly one-third of the space. These little rooms were frightfully warm, because both Afanasii Ivanovich and Pulcheria Ivanovna were fond of heat. All their fuel was stored in the vestibule, which was always filled nearly to the ceiling with straw, which is generally used in Little Russia in the place of wood. The crackling and blaze of burning straw render the ante-rooms extremely pleasant on winter evenings, when some lively youth, chilled with his pursuit of some brunette maid, rushes in, beating his hands together.

The walls of the rooms were adorned with pictures in narrow, old-fashioned frames. I am positive that their owners had long ago forgotten their subjects; and, if some of them had been carried off, they probably would not have noticed it. Two of them were large portraits in oil: one represented some bishop; the other, Peter III. From a narrow frame gazed the Duchess of La Vallière, spotted by flies. Around the windows and above the doors were a multitude of small pictures, which you grow accustomed to regard as spots on the wall, and which you never look at. The floor in nearly all the rooms was of clay, but smoothly plastered down, and more cleanly kept than any polished floor of wood in a wealthy house, languidly swept by a sleepy gentleman in livery. Pulcheria Ivanovna's room was all furnished with chests and boxes, and little chests and little boxes. A multitude of little packages and bags, containing seeds—flower-seeds, vegetable-seeds, watermelon-seeds—hung on the walls. A great many balls of various colored woollens, scraps of old dresses, sewed together during half a century, were stuffed away in the corners, in the chests, and between the chests. Pulcheria Ivanovna was a famous housewife, and saved up every thing; though she sometimes did not know herself what use she could ever make of it.

But the most noticeable thing about the house was the singing doors. Just as soon as day arrived, the songs of the doors resounded throughout the house. I cannot say why they sang. Either the rusty hinges were the cause, or else the mechanic who made them concealed some secret in them; but it was worthy of note, that each door had its own particular voice: the door leading to the bedroom sang the thinnest of sopranos; the dining-room door growled a bass; but the one which led into the vestibule gave out a strange, quavering, yet groaning sound, so that, if you listened to it, you heard at last, quite clearly, "Batiushka [Little Father], I am freezing." I know that this noise is very displeasing to many, but I am very fond of it; and if I chance to hear a door squeak here, I seem to see the country; the low-ceiled chamber, lighted by a candle in an old-fashioned candlestick; the supper on the table; May darkness; night peeping in from the garden through the open windows upon the table set with dishes; the nightingale, which floods the garden, house, and the distant river with her trills; the rustle and the murmuring of the boughs, . . . and, O God! what a long chain of reminiscences is woven!

The chairs in the room were of wood, and massive, in the style which generally distinguished those of olden times; all had high, turned backs of natural wood, without any paint or varnish; they were not even upholstered, and somewhat resembled those which are still used by bishops. Three-cornered tables stood in the corners, a square one before the sofa; and there was a large mirror in a thin gold frame, carved in leaves, which the flies had covered with black spots; in front of the sofa was a mat with flowers resembling birds, and birds resembling flowers. And this constituted nearly the whole furniture of the far from elegant little house where my old people lived. The maids' room was filled with young and elderly serving-women in striped petticoats, to whom Pulcheria Ivanovna sometimes gave some trifles to sew, and whom she made pick over berries, but who ran about the kitchen or slept the greater part of the time. Pulcheria Ivanovna regarded it as a necessity to keep them in the house; and she looked strictly after their morals, but to no purpose.

Upon the window-panes buzzed a terrible number of flies, overpowered by the heavy bass of the bumble-bee, sometimes accompanied by the penetrating shriek of the wasp; but, as soon as the candles were brought in, this whole horde betook themselves to their night quarters, and covered the entire ceiling with a black cloud.

Afanasii Ivanovich very rarely occupied himself with the farming; although he sometimes went out to the mowers and reapers, and gazed quite intently at their work. All the burden of management devolved upon Pulcheria Ivanovna. Pulcheria Ivanovna's house-keeping consisted of an incessant unlocking and locking of the storeroom, in salting, drying, preserving innumerable quantities of fruits and vegetables. Her house was exactly like a chemical laboratory. A fire was constantly laid under the apple-tree; and the kettle or the brass pan with preserves, jelly, marmalade—made with honey, with sugar, and I know not with what else—was hardly ever removed from the tripod. Under another tree the coachman was forever distilling vodka with peach-leaves, with wild cherry, cherry-flowers, gentian, or cherry-stones in a copper still; and, at the end of the process, he never was able to control his tongue, chattered all sorts of nonsense, which Pulcheria Ivanovna did not understand, and took himself off to the kitchen to sleep. Such a quantity of all this stuff was preserved, salted, and dried, that it would probably have overwhelmed the whole yard at last (for Pulcheria Ivanovna loved to lay in a store beyond what was calculated for consumption), if the greater part of it had not been devoured by the maid-servants, who crept into the storeroom, and over-ate themselves to such a fearful extent, that they groaned and complained of their stomachs for a whole day afterwards.

It was less possible for Pulcheria Ivanovna to attend to the agricultural department. The steward conspired with the village elder to rob in the most shameless manner. They had got into a habit of going to their master's forest as though to their own; they manufactured a lot of sledges, and sold them at the neighboring fair; besides which they sold all the stout oaks to the neighboring Cossacks for beams, for a mill. Only once Pulcheria Ivanovna wished to inspect her forest. For this purpose the droshky, with its huge leather apron, was harnessed. As soon as the coachman shook his reins, and the horses (which had served in the militia) started, it filled the air with strange sounds, as though fifes, tambourines, and drums were suddenly audible: every nail and iron bolt rattled so, that, when the pani [mistress] drove from the door, they could be heard clear to the mill, although that was not less than two versts* away. Pulcheria Ivanovna could not fail to observe the terrible havoc in the forest, and the loss of oaks which she recollected from her childhood as being centuries old.

"Why have the oaks become so scarce, Nichípor?" she said to the steward, who was also present. "See that the hairs on your head do not become scarce."

"Why are they scarce?" said the steward. "They disappeared, they disappeared altogether: the lightning struck them, and the worms ate them. They disappeared, pani, they disappeared."

Pulcheria Ivanovna was quite satisfied with this answer, and on returning home merely gave orders that double guards should be placed over the Spanish cherries and the large winter-pear trees in the garden.

These worthy managers—the steward and the village elder—considered it quite unnecessary to bring all the flour to the storehouses at the manor, and that half was quite sufficient for the masters, and finally, that half was brought sprinkled or wet through—what had been rejected at the fair. But no matter how the steward and village elder plundered, or how horribly they devoured things at the house, from the housekeeper down to the pigs, who not only made way with frightful quantities of plums and apples, but even shook the trees with their snouts in order to bring down a whole shower of fruit; no matter how the sparrows and crows pecked, or how many presents the servants carried to their friends in other villages, including even old linen and yarn from the storeroom, which all brought up eventually at the universal source, namely, the tavern; no matter how guests, phlegmatic coachmen, and lackeys stole—yet the fruitful earth yielded such an abundance, Afanasii Ivanovich and Pulcheria Ivanovna needed so little, that all this abominable robbery seemed to pass quite unperceived in their household.

Both the old folks, in accordance with old-fashioned customs, were very fond of eating. As soon as daylight dawned (they always rose early), and the doors had begun their many-toned concert, they seated themselves at table, and drank coffee. When Afanasii Ivanovich had drunk his coffee, he went out, and, flirting his handkerchief, said, "Kish, kish! go away from the veranda, geese!" In the yard he generally encountered the steward; he usually entered into conversation with him, inquired about

* [A verst is about ³/₅ of a mile.—EDITOR, 1992.]

the work with the greatest minuteness, and communicated such a number of observations and orders as would have caused any one to wonder at his knowledge of affairs; and no novice would have ventured to suppose that such an acute master could be robbed. But his steward was a clever rascal: he knew well what answers it was necessary to give, and, better still, how to manage things.

After this, Afanasii Ivanovich returned to the room, and said, approaching Pulcheria Ivanovna, "Well, Pulcheria Ivanovna, is it time to eat something, perhaps?"

"What shall we have to eat now, Afanasii Ivanovich—some wheat and tallow cakes, or some pies with poppy-seeds, or some salted mushrooms?"

"Some mushrooms, then, if you please, or some pies," replied Afanasii Ivanovich; and then suddenly a table-cloth would make its appearance on the table, with the pies and mushrooms.

An hour before dinner, Afanasii Ivanovich took another snack, and drank vodka from an ancient silver cup, ate mushrooms, divers dried fish, and other things. They sat down to dine at twelve o'clock. Besides the dishes and sauce-boats, there stood upon the table a multitude of pots with covers pasted on, that the appetizing products of the savory old-fashioned cooking might not be exhaled abroad. At dinner the conversation turned upon subjects closely connected with the meal.

"It seems to me," Afanasii Ivanovich generally observed, "that this groats is burned a little. Does it strike you so, Pulcheria Ivanovna?"

"No, Afanasii Ivanovich: put on a little more butter, and then it will not taste burned; or take this mushroom sauce, and pour over it."

"If you please," said Afanasii Ivanovich, handing his plate, "let us see how that will do."

After dinner Afanasii Ivanovich went to lie down for an hour, after which Pulcheria Ivanovna brought him a sliced watermelon, and said, "Here, try this, Afanasii Ivanovich; see what a good melon it is."

"Don't trust it because it is red in the centre, Pulcheria Ivanovna," said Afanasii Ivanovich, taking a good-sized chunk. "Sometimes they are red, but not good."

But the watermelon slowly disappeared. Then Afanasii Ivanovich ate a few pears, and went out for a walk in the garden with Pulcheria Ivanovna. On returning to the house, Pulcheria went about her own affairs; but he sat down on the veranda facing the yard, and observed how the store-room's interior was constantly disclosed, and again concealed; and how the girls jostled one another as they carried in, or brought out, all sorts of stuff in wooden boxes, sieves, trays, and other receptacles for fruit. After waiting a while, he sent for Pulcheria Ivanovna, or went to her himself, and said, "What is there for me to eat, Pulcheria Ivanovna?"

"What is there?" said Pulcheria Ivanovna: "shall I go and tell them to bring you some berry tarts which I had set aside for you?"

"That would be good," replied Afanasii Ivanovich.

"Or perhaps you could eat some kissel [sour jelly]?"

"That is good too," replied Afanasii Ivanovich; whereupon all was brought immediately, and eaten in due course.

Before supper Afanasii Ivanovich took another snack. At half-past nine they sat down to supper. After supper they went directly to bed, and universal silence settled down upon this busy yet quiet nook.

The chamber in which Afanasii Ivanovich and Pulcheria Ivanovna slept was so hot that very few people could have stayed in it more than a few hours; but Afanasii Ivanovich, for the sake of more warmth, slept upon the stove-bench, although the excessive heat caused him to rise several times in the course of the night, and walk about the room. Sometimes Afanasii Ivanovich groaned as he walked about the room.

Then Pulcheria Ivanovna inquired, "Why do you groan, Afanasii Ivanovich?"

"God knows, Pulcheria Ivanovna! it seems as if my stomach ached a little," said Afanasii Ivanovich.

"Hadn't you better eat something, Afanasii Ivanovich?"

"I don't know—perhaps it would be well, Pulcheria Ivanovna. By the way, what is there to eat?"

"Sour milk, or some stewed dried pears."

"If you please, I will try them," said Afanasii Ivanovich. The sleepy maid was sent to ransack the cupboards, and Afanasii Ivanovich ate a plateful; after which he remarked, "Now I seem to feel relieved."

Sometimes when the weather was clear, and the rooms were very much heated, Afanasii Ivanovich got merry, and loved to tease Pulcheria Ivanovna, and talk of something out of the ordinary.

"Well, Pulcheria Ivanovna," he said, "what if our house were to suddenly burn down, what would become of us?"

"God forbid!" ejaculated Pulcheria Ivanovna, crossing herself.

"Well, now, just suppose a case, that our house should burn down. Where should we go then?"

"God knows what you are saying, Afanasii Ivanovich! How could our house burn down? God will not permit that."

"Well, but if it did burn?"

"Well, then, we should go to the kitchen. You could occupy for a time the room which the housekeeper now has."

"But if the kitchen burned too?"

"The idea! God will preserve us from such a catastrophe as the house and the kitchen both burning down. In that case, we could go into the store-house while a new house was being built."

"And if the store-house burned also?"

"God knows what you are saying! I won't listen to you! it is a sin to talk so, and God will punish you for such speeches."

But Afanasii Ivanovich, content with having had his joke over Pulcheria Ivanovna, sat quietly in his chair, and smiled.

But the old people were most interesting of all to me when they had visitors. Then everything about their house assumed a different aspect. It may be said that these good people only lived for their guests. They vied with each other in offering you everything which the place produced. But the most pleasing feature of it all to me was, that, in all their kindliness, there was nothing feigned. Their kindness and readiness to oblige were so gently expressed in their faces, so became them, that you involuntarily yielded to their requests. These were the outcome of the pure, clear simplicity of their good, sincere souls. Their joy was not at all of the sort with which the official of the court favors you, when he has become a personage through your exertions, and calls you his benefactor, and fawns at your feet. No guest was ever permitted to depart on the day of his arrival: he must needs pass the night with them.

"How is it possible to set out at so late an hour upon so long a journey!" Pulcheria Ivanovna always observed. (The visitor usually lived three or four versts from them.)

"Of course," said Afanasii Ivanovich, "it is impossible on all accounts: robbers, or some other evil men, will attack you."

"May God in his mercy deliver us from robbers!" said Pulcheria Ivanovna. "And why mention such things at night? Robbers, or no robbers, it is dark, and no fit time to travel. And your coachman, . . . I know your coachman: he is so weak and small, any horse could kill him; besides, he has probably been drinking, and is now asleep somewhere."

And the visitor was obliged to remain. But the evening in the warm, low room, cheerful, strewn with stories, the steam rising from the food upon the table, which was always nourishing, and cooked in a masterly manner—this was his reward. I seem now to see Afanasii Ivanovich bending to seat himself at the table, with his constant smile, and listening with attention, and even with delight, to his guest. The conversation often turned on politics. The guest, who also emerged but rarely from his village, frequently with significant mien and mysterious expression of countenance, aired his surmises, and told how the French had formed a secret compact with the English to let Buonaparte loose upon Russia again, or talked merely of the impending war; and then Afanasii Ivanovich often remarked, without appearing to look at Pulcheria Ivanovna:

"I am thinking of going to the war myself. Why cannot I go to the war?"

"You have been already," broke in Pulcheria Ivanovna. "Don't believe him," she said, turning to the visitor; "what good would he, an old man, do in the war? The very first soldier would shoot him; by Heaven, he would shoot him! he would take aim, and fire at him."

"What?" said Afanasii Ivanovich. "I would shoot him."

"Just listen to him!" interposed Pulcheria Ivanovna. "Why should he go to the war? And his pistols have been rusty this long time, and are lying in the storeroom. If you could only see them! the powder would burst them before they would fire. He will blow his hands off, and disfigure his face, and be miserable forever after!"

"What's that?" said Afanasii Ivanovich. "I will buy myself new arms: I will take my sword or a Cossack lance."

"These are all inventions: as soon as a thing comes into his head, he begins to talk about it!" interrupted Pulcheria Ivanovna with vexation. "I know that he is jesting, but it is unpleasant to hear him all the same. He always talks so; sometimes you listen and listen, until it is perfectly frightful."

But Afanasii Ivanovich, satisfied with having frightened Pulcheria Ivanovna, laughed as he sat doubled up in his chair.

Pulcheria Ivanovna seemed to me most noteworthy when she offered her guest zakuska.* "Here," she said, taking the cork from a decanter, "is genuine yarrow or sage vodka; if any one's shoulder-blades or loins ache, this is a very good remedy: here is some with gentian; if you have a ringing in your ears, or eruption on your face, this is very good: and this is distilled with peach-kernels; here, take a glass; what a fine perfume! If ever any one, in getting out of bed, strikes himself against the corner of the clothes-press or table, and a bump comes on his forehead, all he has to do is to drink a glass of this before meals—and it all disappears out of hand, as though it had never been."

Then followed a catalogue of the other decanters, almost all of which possessed some healing properties. Having loaded down her guest with this complete apothecary shop, she led him to where a multitude of dishes were set out. "Here are mushrooms with summer-savory; and here are some with cloves and walnuts. A Turkish woman taught me how to pickle them, at a time when there were still Turkish prisoners among us. She was a good Turk, and it was not noticeable that she professed the Turkish faith: she behaved very nearly as we do, only she would not eat pork; they say that it is forbidden by their laws. Here are mushrooms with currant-leaves and nutmeg; and here, some with clove-pinks. These are the first I have cooked in vinegar. I don't know how good they are. I learned the secret from Ivan's father: you must first spread oak-leaves in a

---

* A whet to the appetite preliminary to dinner, consisting of caviare, herring, smoked salmon, sardines, smoked goose, sausages, cheese-bread, butter, vodka, etc.—TRANSLATOR.

small cask, and then sprinkle on pepper and saltpetre, and then more, until it becomes the color of hawk-weed, and then spread the liquid over the mushrooms. And here are cheese-tarts; these are different: and here are some pies with cabbage and buckwheat flour, which Afanasii Ivanovich is extremely fond of."

"Yes," added Afanasii Ivanovich, "I am very fond of them: they are soft and a little tart."

Pulcheria Ivanovna was generally in very good spirits when they had visitors. Good old woman! she belonged entirely to her guests. I loved to stay with them; and though I over-ate myself horribly, like all who visited them, and although it was very bad for me, still, I was always glad to go to them. Besides, I think the air of Little Russia must possess some special properties which aid digestion; for if any one undertook to eat here, in that way, there is no doubt but that he would find himself lying on the table instead of in bed.

Good old people! . . . But my story approaches a very sad event, which changed forever the life in that peaceful nook. This event appears all the more striking because it resulted from the most insignificant cause. But, in accordance with the primitive arrangement of things, the most trifling causes produce the greatest events, and the grandest undertakings end in the most insignificant results. Some warrior collects all the forces of his empire, fights for several years, his colonels distinguish themselves, and at last it all ends in the acquisition of a bit of land on which no one would even plant potatoes; but sometimes, on the other hand, a couple of sausage-makers in different towns quarrel over some trifle, and the quarrel at last extends to the towns, and then to the villages and hamlets, and then to the whole empire. But we will drop these reflections; they lead nowhere: and, besides, I am not fond of reflections when they remain mere reflections.

Pulcheria Ivanovna had a little gray cat, which almost always lay coiled up in a ball at her feet. Pulcheria Ivanovna stroked her occasionally, and with her finger tickled her neck, which the petted cat stretched out as long as possible. It was impossible to say that Pulcheria Ivanovna loved her so very much, but she had simply become attached to her from having become used to seeing her about continually. But Afanasii Ivanovich often joked at such an attachment.

"I cannot see, Pulcheria Ivanovna, what you find attractive in that cat; of what use is she? If you had a dog, that would be quite another thing; you can take a dog out hunting, but what is a cat good for?"

"Be quiet, Afanasii Ivanovich," said Pulcheria Ivanovna: "you just like to talk, and that's all. A dog is not clean; a dog soils things, and breaks everything: but the cat is a peaceable beast; she does no harm to any one."

But it made no difference to Afanasii Ivanovich whether it was a cat or a dog; he only said it to tease Pulcheria Ivanovna.

Behind their garden was a large wood, which had been spared by the enterprising steward, possibly because the sound of the axe might have reached the ears of Pulcheria Ivanovna. It was dense, neglected: the old tree-trunks were concealed by luxuriant hazel-bushes, and resembled the feathered legs of pigeons. In this wood dwelt wild-cats. The wild forest-cats must not be confounded with those which run about the roofs of houses: being in the city, they are much more civilized, in spite of their savage nature, than the denizens of the woods. These, on the contrary, are mostly fierce and wild: they are always lean and ugly, and miauw in rough, untutored voices. They sometimes scratch for themselves underground passages to the store-houses, and steal tallow. They occasionally make their appearance in the kitchen, springing suddenly in at an open window, when they see that the cook has gone off among the grass. As a rule, noble feelings are unknown to them: they live by thievery, and strangle the little sparrows in their very nests. These cats had a long conference with Pulcheria Ivanovna's tame cat, through a hole under the store-house, and finally led her astray, as a detachment of soldiers leads astray a dull peasant. Pulcheria Ivanovna noticed that her cat was missing, and sent to look for her; but no cat was to be found. Three days passed: Pulcheria Ivanovna felt sorry, but finally forgot all about her loss.

One day she had been inspecting her vegetable-garden, and was returning with her hands full of fresh green cucumbers, which she had picked for Afanasii Ivanovich, when a most pitiful miauwing struck her ear. She instinctively called, "Kitty! kitty!" and out from the tall grass came her gray cat, thin and starved. It was evident that she had not had a mouthful of food for days. Pulcheria Ivanovna continued to call her; but the cat stood crying before her, and did not venture to approach. It was plain that she had become quite wild in that time. Pulcheria Ivanovna stepped forward, still calling the cat, which followed her timidly to the fence. Finally, seeing familiar places, it entered the room.

Pulcheria Ivanovna at once ordered milk and meat to be given her, and, sitting down by her, enjoyed the avidity with which her poor pet swallowed morsel after morsel, and lapped the milk. The gray runaway fattened before her very eyes, and began to eat less eagerly. Pulcheria Ivanovna reached out her hand to stroke her; but the ungrateful animal had evidently become too well used to robber cats, or adopted some romantic notion about love and poverty being better than a palace, for the cats were as poor as church-mice. However that may be, she sprang through the window, and none of the servants were able to catch her.

The old woman reflected. "It is my death which has come for me," she said to herself; and nothing could cheer her. All day she was sad. In vain did Afanasii Ivanovich jest, and want to know why she had suddenly grown so grave. Pulcheria Ivanovna either made no reply, or one which was in no way satisfactory to Afanasii Ivanovich. The next day she was visibly thinner.

"What is the matter with you, Pulcheria Ivanovna? You are not ill?"

"No, I am not ill, Afanasii Ivanovich. I want to tell you about a strange occurrence. I know that I shall die this year: my death has already come for me."

Afanasii Ivanovich's mouth became distorted with pain. Nevertheless, he tried to conquer the sad feeling in his mind, and said, smiling, "God only knows what you are talking about, Pulcheria Ivanovna! You must have drunk some peach infusion instead of your usual herb-tea."

"No, Afanasii Ivanovich, I have not drunk the peach," said Pulcheria Ivanovna.

And Afanasii Ivanovich was sorry that he had made fun of Pulcheria Ivanovna; and, as he looked at her, a tear hung on his lashes.

"I beg you, Afanasii Ivanovich, to fulfil my wishes," said Pulcheria Ivanovna. "When I die, bury me by the church-wall. Put my grayish dress on me—the one with small flowers on a cinnamon ground. My satin dress with red stripes, you must not put on me; a corpse needs no clothes. Of what use are they to her? But it will be good for you. Make yourself a fine dressing-gown, in case visitors come, so that you can make a good appearance when you receive them."

"God knows what you are saying, Pulcheria Ivanovna!" said Afanasii Ivanovich. "Death will come some time, but you frighten one with such remarks."

"No, Afanasii Ivanovich: I know when my death is to be. But do not sorrow for me. I am old, and stricken in years; and you, too, are old. We shall soon meet in the other world."

But Afanasii Ivanovich sobbed like a child.

"It is a sin to weep, Afanasii Ivanovich. Do not sin and anger God by your grief. I am not sorry to die: I am only sorry for one thing"—a heavy sob broke her speech for a moment—"I am sorry because I do not know whom I shall leave with you, who will look after you when I am dead. You are like a little child: the one who attends you must love you." And her face expressed such deep and heart-felt sorrow, that I do not know whether any one could have beheld her, and remained unmoved.

"Mind, Yavdokha," she said, turning to the housekeeper, whom she had ordered to be summoned expressly, "that you look after your master when I am dead, and cherish him like the apple of your eye, like your own child. See that everything he likes is prepared in the kitchen; that his linen and clothes are always clean; that, when visitors happen in, you dress him properly: otherwise he will come forth in his old dressing-gown, for he often forgets now whether it is a festival or an ordinary day. Do not take your eyes off him, Yavdokha. I will pray for you in the other world, and God will reward you. Do not forget, Yavdokha. You are old— you have not long to live. Take no sins upon your soul. If you do not look well to him, you will have no happiness in the world. I will beg God myself to give you an unhappy ending. And you will be unhappy yourself, and your children will be unhappy; and none of your race will ever have God's blessing."

Poor old woman! she thought not of the great moment which awaited her, nor of her soul, nor of the future life: she thought only of her poor companion, with whom she had passed her life, and whom she was leaving an orphan and unprotected. After this fashion, she arranged everything with great skill: so that, after her death, Afanasii Ivanovich might not perceive her absence. Her faith in her approaching end was so firm, and her mind was so fixed upon it, that, in a few days, she actually took to her bed, and was unable to take any nourishment.

Afanasii Ivanovich was all attention, and never left her bedside. "Perhaps you could eat something, Pulcheria Ivanovna," he said, looking uneasily into her eyes. But Pulcheria Ivanovna made no reply. At length, after a long silence, she moved her lips, as though desirous of saying something—and her breath fled.

Afanasii Ivanovich was utterly amazed. It seemed to him so terrible, that he did not even weep. He gazed at her with troubled eyes, as though he did not comprehend the meaning of a corpse.

They laid the dead woman on a table, dressed her in the dress she herself had designated, crossed her arms, and placed a wax candle in her hand. He looked on without feeling. A throng of people of every class filled the court. Long tables were spread in the yard, and covered with heaps of *kutya*,* fruit-wine, and pies. The visitors talked, wept, looked at the dead woman, discussed her qualities, gazed at him; but he looked upon it all as a stranger might. At last they carried out the dead woman: the people thronged after, and he followed. The priests were in full vestments, the sun shone, the infants cried in their mothers' arms, the larks sang, the children in their little blouses ran and capered along the road. Finally they placed the coffin over the grave. They bade him approach and kiss the dead woman for the last time. He approached, and kissed her. Tears appeared in his eyes, but unfeeling tears. The coffin was lowered: the priest took the shovel, and flung in the first earth. The full choir of deacons and two sacristans sang the requiem under the blue, cloudless sky. The laborers grasped their shovels; and the grave was soon filled, the earth levelled off. Then he pressed forward. All stood aside to

---

* Rice cooked with honey and raisins.—TRANSLATOR.

make room for him, wishing to know his object. He raised his eyes, looked about in a bewildered way, and said, "And so you have buried her! Why?"— He paused, and did not finish his sentence.

But when he returned home, when he saw that his chamber was empty, that even the chair on which Pulcheria Ivanovna was wont to sit had been carried out, he sobbed, sobbed violently, irrepressibly; and tears ran in streams from his dim eyes.

Five years passed. What grief will time not efface! What passion is not cured in unequal battle with it! I knew a man in the bloom of his youthful strength, full of true nobility and worth; I knew that he loved, tenderly, passionately, wildly, boldly, modestly; and in my presence, before my very eyes, almost, the object of his passion—a girl, gentle, beautiful as an angel—was struck by insatiable Death. I never beheld such a terrible outburst of spiritual suffering, such mad, fiery grief, such consuming despair, as agitated the unfortunate lover. I never thought that a man could make for himself such a hell, where there was neither shadow nor form, nor any thing in any way resembling hope. . . . They tried never to let him out of sight: they concealed all weapons from him by which he could commit suicide. Two weeks later he regained control of himself; he began to laugh and jest; they gave him his freedom, and the first use he made of it was to buy a pistol. One day a sudden shot startled his relatives terribly: they rushed into the room, and beheld him stretched out, with his skull crushed. A physician who chanced to be present, and who enjoyed a universal reputation for skill, discovered some signs of life in him, found that the wound was not fatal; and he was cured, to the great amazement of all. The watchfulness over him was redoubled; even at table, they never put a knife near him, and tried to keep everything away from him with which he could injure himself. But he soon found a fresh opportunity, and threw himself under the wheels of a passing carriage. His hand and feet were crushed, but again he was cured. A year after this I saw him in a crowded *salon*. He was talking gayly, as he covered a card; and behind him, leaning upon the back of his chair, stood his young wife, turning over his counters.

Being in the vicinity during the course of the five years already mentioned, which succeeded Pulcheria Ivanovna's death, I went to the little farm of Afanasii Ivanovich, to inquire after my old neighbor, with whom I had formerly spent the day so agreeably, dining always on the choicest delicacies of his kind-hearted wife. When I drove up to the door, the house seemed twice as old; the peasants' izbás were lying completely on one side, without doubt, exactly like their owners; the fence and hedge around the courtyard were completely dilapidated; and I myself saw the cook pull out a paling to heat the stove, when she had only a couple of steps to take in order to get the kindling-wood which had been piled there expressly. I stepped sadly upon the veranda: the same dogs, now blind, or with broken legs, raised their bushy tails, all matted with burs, and barked.

The old man came out to meet me. So, this was he! I recognized him at once, but he was twice as bent as formerly. He knew me, and greeted me with the smile already so well known to me. I followed him into the room. All there seemed the same as in the past; but I observed a sort of strange disorder, a tangible absence of something: in a word, I experienced that strange sensation which takes possession of us when we enter, for the first time, the dwelling of a widower whom we had heretofore known as inseparable from the companion who has been with him all his life. This sensation resembles the one we feel when we see before us a man whom we had always known as healthy, without his legs. In everything was visible the absence of painstaking Pulcheria Ivanovna. At table they gave us a knife without a handle: the dishes were not prepared with so much art. I did not care to inquire about the management of the estate: I was even afraid to glance at the farm-buildings.

When we sat down at the table, a maid fastened a napkin in front of Afanasii Ivanovich; and it was very well that she did so, for otherwise he would have spotted his dressing-gown all over with gravy. I tried to interest him in something, and told him various bits of news. He listened with his usual smile, but his glance was at times quite unintelligent; and thoughts did not wander there, but only disappeared. He frequently raised a spoonful of porridge, and, instead of carrying it to his mouth, carried it to his nose; and, instead of sticking his fork into the chicken, he struck the decanter with it; and then the servant, taking his hand, guided it to the chicken. We sometimes waited several minutes for the next course. Afanasii Ivanovich remarked it himself, and said, "Why are they so long in bringing the food?" But I saw through a crack of the door that the boy who brought the dishes was not thinking of it at all, but was fast asleep, with his head leaning on a stool.

"This is the dish," said Afanasii Ivanovich, when they brought us *mnishki* [curds and flour] with cream—"this is the dish," he continued, and I observed that his voice began to quiver, and that tears were ready to peep from his leaden eyes; but he collected all his strength, striving to repress them: "This is the dish which the—the—the de—ceas"—and the tears suddenly burst forth: his hand fell upon the plate, the plate was overturned, flew from the table, and was broken; the gravy ran all over him. He sat stupidly holding his spoon, and tears like a never-ceasing fountain flowed, flowed in streams down upon his napkin.

"O God!" I thought, as I looked at him, "five years of all-obliterating time, . . . an old man, an already apathetic old man, who, in all his life, apparently, was never agitated by any strong spiritual emotion, whose whole life seemed to consist in sitting on a high chair, in eating dried fish and pears, in telling good-natured stories—and yet so long and fervent a grief! Which wields the most powerful sway over us, passion or habit? Or are all our strong impulses, all the whirlwinds of our desire and boiling passions, but the consequence of our fierce young growth, and only for that reason seem deep and annihilating?" However that may be, all our passion, on that occasion, seemed to me child's play beside this long, slow, almost insensible habit. Several times he tried to pronounce the dead woman's name; but in the middle of the word his peaceful and ordinary face became convulsively distorted, and a childlike fit of weeping cut me to the heart.

No: these were not the tears of which old people are generally so lavish, when representing to us their wretched condition and unhappiness. Neither were these the tears which they drop over a glass of punch. No: these were tears which flowed without asking a reason, distilled from the bitter pain of a heart already growing cold.

He did not live long after this. I heard of his death recently. It was strange, though, that the circumstances attending his death somewhat resembled those of Pulcheria Ivanovna's. One day Afanasii Ivanovich decided to take a short stroll in the garden. As he went slowly down the path, with his usual carelessness, a strange thing happened to him. All at once he heard some one behind him say, in a distinct voice, "Afanasii Ivanovich." He turned round, but there was no one there. He looked on all sides: he peered into the shrubbery—no one anywhere. The day was calm, and the sun shone clear. He pondered for a moment. His face lighted up; and at length he exclaimed, "It is Pulcheria Ivanovna calling me!"

It has doubtless happened to you, at some time or other, to hear a voice calling you by name, which the peasants explain by saying that a man's spirit is longing for him, and calls him, and that death inevitably follows. I confess that this mysterious call has always been very terrifying to *me*. I remember to have often heard it in my childhood. Sometimes some one suddenly pronounced my name distinctly behind me. The day, on such occasions, was usually bright and sunny. Not a leaf on a tree moved. The silence was deathlike: even the grasshoppers had ceased to whir. There was not a soul in the garden. But I must confess, that, if the wildest and most stormy night, with the utmost inclemency of the elements, had overtaken me alone in the midst of an impassable forest, I should not have been so much alarmed by it as by this fearful stillness amid a cloudless day. On such occasions, I usually ran in the greatest terror, catching my breath, from the garden, and only regained composure when I encountered some person, the sight of whom dispelled the terrible inward solitude.

He yielded himself up utterly to his moral conviction that Pulcheria Ivanovna was calling him. He yielded with the will of a submissive child, withered away, coughed, melted away like a candle, and at length expired like it, when nothing remains to feed its poor flame. "Lay me beside Pulcheria Ivanovna"—that was all he said before his death.

His wish was fulfilled; and they buried him beside the church, close to Pulcheria Ivanovna's grave. The guests at the funeral were few, but there was a throng of common and poor people. The house was already quite deserted. The enterprising clerk and village elder carried off to their izbás all the old household utensils and things which the housekeeper did not manage to appropriate.

There shortly appeared, from some unknown quarter, a distant relative, the heir of the property, who had served as lieutenant in some regiment, I forget which, and was a great reformer. He immediately perceived the great waste and neglect in the management. This decided him to root out, re-arrange, and introduce order into everything. He purchased six fine English scythes, nailed a number on each izbá, and finally managed so well, that in six months the estate was in the hands of trustees. The wise trustees (consisting of an ex-assessor and a captain of the staff in faded uniform) promptly carried off all the hens and eggs. The izbás, nearly all of which were lying on the ground, fell into complete ruin. The muzhiks wandered off, and were mostly numbered among the runaways. The real owner himself (who lived on peaceable terms with his trustees, and drank punch with them) very rarely entered his village, and did not long live there. From that time forth, he has been going about to all the fairs in Little Russia, carefully inquiring prices at various large establishments, which sell at wholesale, flour, hemp, honey, and so forth, but he buys only the smallest trifles, such as a flint, a nail to clean his pipe, or anything, the value of which at wholesale does not exceed a ruble.

The Tale
of How Ivan Ivanovich Quarrelled with Ivan Nikiforovich

I.

IVAN IVANOVICH AND IVAN NIKIFOROVICH.

A FINE BEKESHA [short shooting-coat] has Ivan Ivanovich! splendid! And what lambskin! deuce take it, what lambskin! blue-black with silver lights. I'll forfeit, I know not what, if you find any one else owning any such. Look at it, for Heaven's sake, especially when he stands talking with any one! look at him from the side: what a pleasure it is! To describe it, is impossible: velvet! silver! fire! Heavens! Nikolai the Wonder-worker, saint of God! why have not I such a bekesha? He had it made before Agafya Fedosyevna went to Kief. You know Agafya Fedosyevna, the same who bit the assessor's ear off.

Ivan Ivanovich was a very handsome man. What a house he had in Mirgorod! Around it on every side was a veranda on oaken pillars, and on the veranda everywhere were benches. Ivan Ivanovich, when the weather gets too warm, throws off his bekesha and his underclothing, remains in his shirt alone, and rests on the veranda, and observes what is going on in the court-yard and the street. What apples and pears he has under his very windows! You have but to open the window, and the branches force themselves through into the room. All this is in front of the house; but you should have seen what he had in the garden. What was there not there? Plums, cherries, black-hearts, every sort of vegetable, sunflowers, cucumbers, melons, peas, a threshing-floor, and even a forge.

A very fine man, Ivan Ivanovich! He is very fond of melons: they

19

are his favorite food. Just as soon as he has dined, and come out on his veranda, in his shirt, he orders Gapka to fetch two melons, and immediately cuts them himself, collects the seeds in a paper, and begins to eat. Then he orders Gapka to fetch the ink-bottle, and, with his own hand, writes this inscription on the paper of seeds: *These melons were eaten on such and such a date.* If there was a guest present, then it reads, *Such and such a person assisted.*

The late judge of Mirgorod always gazed at Ivan Ivanovich's house with pleasure. Yes, the little house was very pretty. It pleased me because sheds, and still other little sheds, were built on to it on all sides; so that, looking at it from a distance, only roofs were visible, rising one above another, which greatly resembled a plate full of pancakes, or, better still, fungi growing on the trunk of a tree. Moreover, the roofs were all overgrown with weeds: a willow, an oak, and two apple-trees leaned their spreading branches against it. Through the trees peeped little windows with carved and whitewashed shutters, which projected even into the street.

A very fine man, Ivan Ivanovich! The commissioner of Poltava knows him also. Dorosh Tarasovich Pukhívochka, when he leaves Khorola, always goes to his house. And Father Peter, the Protopope who lives in Koliberda, when he invites a few guests, always says that he knows of no one who so well fulfils all his Christian duties, and understands so well how to live, as Ivan Ivanovich.

How time flies! More than ten years have already passed since he became a widower. He never had any children. Gapka has children, and they run about the court-yard. Ivan Ivanovich always gives each one of them either a round cake, or a slice of melon, or a pear.

Gapka carries the keys of his storerooms and cellars; but the key of the large chest which stands in his bedroom, and that of the centre store-room, Ivan Ivanovich keeps himself; and he does not like to admit any one. Gapka is a healthy girl, and goes about in coarse cloth garments with ruddy cheeks and calves.

And what a pious man is Ivan Ivanovich! Every Sunday he dons his bekesha, and goes to church. On entering, Ivan Ivanovich bows on all sides, generally stations himself in the choir, and sings a very good bass. When the service is over, Ivan Ivanovich cannot refrain from passing the poor people in review. He probably would not have cared to undertake this tiresome work, if his natural goodness had not urged him to it. "Good-day, beggar!" he generally said, selecting the most crippled old woman in the most threadbare garment made of patches. "Whence come you, my poor woman?"

"I come from the farm, panochka [master dear]. 'Tis two days since I have eaten or drunk: my own children drove me out."

"Poor soul! why did you come hither?"

"To beg alms, panochka, to see whether some one will not give at least enough for bread."

"Hm! so you want bread?" Ivan Ivanovich generally inquired.

"How should I not want it? I am as hungry as a dog."

"Hm!" replied Ivan Ivanovich usually, "and perhaps you would like butter too?"

"Yes; everything which your kindness will give; I will be content with all."

"Hm! Is butter better than bread?"

"How is a hungry person to choose? Any thing you please, all is good." Thereupon the old woman generally extended her hand.

"Well, go with God's blessing," said Ivan Ivanovich. "Why do you stand there? I'm not beating you." And turning to a second and a third with the same questions, he finally returns home, or goes to drink a little glass of vodka with his neighbor, Ivan Nikiforovich, or the judge, or the chief of police.

Ivan Ivanovich is very fond of receiving presents. This pleases him very much.

A very fine man also is Ivan Nikiforovich. They are such friends as the world never saw. Anton Prokofievich Golopuz, who goes about to this hour in his cinnamon-colored surtout with blue sleeves, and dines every Sunday with the judge, was in the habit of saying that the Devil himself had bound Ivan Ivanovich and Ivan Nikiforovich together with a rope: where one goes, the other follows.

Ivan Nikiforovich was never married. Although it was reported that he was married, it was completely false. I know Ivan Nikiforovich very well, and am able to state that he never even had any intention of marrying. Where do all these scandals originate? In the same way it was rumored that Ivan Nikiforovich was born with a tail! But this invention is so clumsy, and at the same time so horrible and indecent, that I do not even consider it necessary to refute it for the benefit of civilized readers, to whom it is doubtless known that only witches, and very few even of those, have tails. Witches, moreover, belong more to the feminine than to the masculine gender.

In spite of their great friendship, these rare friends were not always agreed between themselves. Their characters can best be known by comparing them. Ivan Ivanovich has the unusual gift of speaking in an extremely pleasant manner. Heavens! How he does speak! The feeling can best be described by comparing it to that which you experience when some one combs your head, or draws his finger softly across your heel. You listen and listen until you drop your head. Pleasant, exceedingly pleasant! like the sleep after a bath. Ivan Nikiforovich, on the contrary, is more reticent; but, if he once takes up the word, look out for yourself! He shaves better than any barber.

Ivan Ivanovich is tall and thin; Ivan Nikiforovich is rather shorter in stature, but he makes it up in thickness. Ivan Ivanovich's head is like a radish, tail down; Ivan Nikiforovich's like a radish with the tail up. Ivan Ivanovich lies on the veranda in his shirt after dinner only: in the evening he dons his bekesha, and goes out somewhere, either to the village store, where he supplies flour, or into the fields to catch quail. Ivan Nikiforovich lies all day on his porch; if the day is not too hot, he generally turns his back to the sun, and will not go anywhere. If it happens to occur to him in the morning, he walks through the yard, inspects the domestic affairs, and retires again to his room.

In early days he used to go to Ivan Ivanovich. Ivan Ivanovich is a very refined man, and in polite conversation never utters an impolite word, and is offended at once if he hears one. Ivan Nikiforovich is not always on his guard. On such occasions Ivan Ivanovich usually rises from his seat, and says, "Enough, enough, Ivan Nikiforovich! it's better to go out into the sun at once, than to utter such godless words."

Ivan Ivanovich goes into a terrible rage if a fly falls into his beet-soup; then he is fairly beside himself; and he flings away his plate, and the housekeeper catches it. Ivan Nikiforovich is exceedingly fond of bathing; and, when he gets up to the neck in water, he orders a table and a *samovar* to be placed on the water, and he is very fond of drinking tea in that cool position. Ivan Ivanovich shaves his beard twice a week; Ivan Nikiforovich, once. Ivan Ivanovich is extremely curious. God preserve you if you begin to tell him anything, and do not finish it! If he is displeased with anything, he lets it be seen at once. It is very hard to tell from Ivan Nikiforovich's countenance whether he is pleased or angry: even if he is rejoiced at anything, he will not show it.

Ivan Ivanovich is of a rather timid character: Ivan Nikiforovich, on the contrary, has such full folds in his trousers, that, if you were to inflate them, you might put the court-yard, with its store-houses and buildings, inside them. Ivan Ivanovich has large, expressive eyes, of a snuff color, and a mouth shaped something like the letter V. Ivan Nikiforovich has small, yellowish eyes, quite concealed between heavy brows and fat cheeks; and his nose is the shape of a ripe plum. If Ivan Ivanovich treats you to snuff, he always licks the cover of his box first with his tongue, then taps on it with his finger, and says, as he raises it, if you are an acquaintance, "Dare I beg you, sir, to give me the pleasure?"—if a stranger, "Dare I beg you, sir, though I have not the honor of knowing your rank, name, and family, to do me the favor?" But Ivan Nikiforovich puts his box straight into your hand, and merely adds, "Do me the favor." Neither Ivan Ivanovich nor Ivan Nikiforovich loves fleas; and therefore, neither Ivan Ivanovich nor Ivan Nikiforovich will, on any account, admit a Jew with his wares, without purchasing of him elixir in various little boxes, as remedies against these insects, having first rated him well for belonging to the Hebrew faith.

But, in spite of numerous dissimilarities, Ivan Ivanovich and Ivan Nikiforovich are both very fine men.

II.

FROM WHICH MAY BE SEEN WHAT IVAN IVANOVICH WANTED, WHENCE AROSE THE DISCUSSION BETWEEN IVAN IVANOVICH AND IVAN NIKIFOROVICH, AND WHERE IT ENDED.

ONE MORNING—it was in July—Ivan Ivanovich was lying on his veranda. The day was warm; the air was dry, and came in gusts. Ivan Ivanovich had been to town, to the mower's, and at the farm, and had succeeded in asking all the muzhiks [peasants] and women whom he met, whence, whither, and why. He was fearfully tired, and had lain down to rest. As he lay there, he looked at the store-houses, the court-yard, the sheds, the chickens running about, and thought to himself, "My Heavens! What a master I am! What is there that I have not? Birds, buildings, granaries, everything I take a fancy to; genuine distilled vodka; pears and plums in the orchard; poppies, cabbages, peas, in the garden; . . . what is there which I have not? I should like to know what there is that I have not?"

As he put this profound question to himself, Ivan Ivanovich reflected; and meantime, his eyes, in their search after fresh objects, crossed the fence into Ivan Nikiforovich's yard, and involuntarily took note of a curious sight. A fat woman was bringing out clothes, which had been packed away, and spreading them out on the line to air. Presently an old uniform with worn trimmings was swinging its sleeves in the air, and embracing a brocade gown; from behind it peeped a court-coat, its buttons stamped with coats-of-arms, and with moth-eaten collar; white cassimere pantaloons with spots, which had once upon a time clothed Ivan Nikiforovich's legs, and might now, possibly, fit his fingers. Behind them were speedily hung some more in the shape of the letter Π. Then came a blue Cossack jacket, which Ivan Nikiforovich had had made twenty years before, when he prepared to enter the militia, and allowed his mustache to grow. And finally, one after another, appeared a sword, projecting into the air like a spit; then the skirts of a grass-green caftan-like garment, with copper buttons the size of a five-kopek piece, unfolded themselves. From among the folds peeped a vest bound with gold, with a wide opening in front. The vest was soon concealed by an old petticoat belonging to his dead grandmother, with pockets which would have held a watermelon. All these things piled together formed a very interesting spectacle for Ivan Ivanovich, while the sun's rays, falling upon bits of a blue or green sleeve, a red binding, or a scrap of gold brocade, or playing on the point of the sword, formed an unusual sight, similar to the representations of the Nativity given at farmhouses by wandering bands; particularly that part where the throng of people, pressing close together, gaze at King Herod in his golden crown, or at Anthony leading his goat: at these exhibitions the fiddle whines, a gypsy taps on his lips in lieu of a drum, and the sun goes down, and the cool freshness of the young night presses more strongly on the shoulders and bosoms of the plump farmers' wives.

Presently the old woman crawled, grunting, from the storeroom, dragging after her an old-fashioned saddle with broken stirrups, worn leather pistol-cases, and saddle-cloth, once red, with gilt embroidery and copper disks.

"Here's a stupid woman," thought Ivan Ivanovich. "She'll be dragging Ivan Nikiforovich out and airing him next."

And with reason: Ivan Ivanovich was not so far wrong in his surmise. Five minutes later, Ivan Nikiforovich's nankeen trousers appeared, and took nearly half the yard to themselves. After that she fetched out a hat and a gun.

"What's the meaning of this?" thought Ivan Ivanovich. "I never saw Ivan Nikiforovich have a gun. What does he want with it? Whether he shoots, or not, he keeps a gun! Of what use is it to him? But it's a splendid thing. I have long wanted to get just such a one; I want that gun very much: I like to amuse myself with a gun. Hello, there, woman, woman!" shouted Ivan Ivanovich, beckoning to her.

The old woman approached the fence.

"What's that you have there, my good woman?"

"A gun, as you see."

"What sort of a gun?"

"Who knows what sort of a gun? If it were mine, perhaps I should know what it is made of; but it is my master's."

Ivan Ivanovich rose, and began to examine the gun on all sides, and forgot to reprove the old woman for hanging it and the sword to air.

"It must be iron," went on the old woman.

"Hm! iron! why iron?" said Ivan Ivanovich to himself. "Has your master had it long?"

"Yes; long, perhaps."

"It's a nice thing!" continued Ivan Ivanovich. "I will ask him for it. What can he do with it? I'll exchange with him for it. Is your master at home, my good woman?"

"Yes."

"What is he doing? lying down?"

"Yes, lying down."

"Very well, I will come to him."

Ivan Ivanovich dressed himself, took his well-seasoned stick for the benefit of the dogs (for, in Mirgorod, there are more dogs than people to be met in the street), and went out.

Although Ivan Nikiforovich's house was next door to Ivan Ivanovich's, so that you could have got from one to the other by climbing the fence, yet Ivan Ivanovich went by the street. From the street it was necessary to turn into an alley which was so narrow, that if two one-horse carts chanced to meet, they could not get out, and were forced to remain there until the drivers, seizing the hind-wheels, dragged them in opposite directions into the street, and pedestrians drew aside like flowers growing by the fence on either hand. Ivan Ivanovich's wagon-shed adjoined this alley on one side; and on the other, Ivan Nikiforovich's granary, gate, and pigeon-house.

Ivan Ivanovich went up to the gate, and rattled the latch. Within arose the barking of dogs; but the motley-haired pack ran back, wagging their tails, when they saw the well-known face. Ivan Ivanovich traversed the court-yard, in which were collected Indian doves fed by Ivan Nikiforovich's own hand, watermelon, and melon-rinds, vegetables, broken wheels, barrel-hoops, or a wallowing small boy with dirty blouse—a picture such as painters love. The shadows of the fluttering clothes covered nearly the whole of the yard, and lent it a degree of coolness. The woman greeted him with an inclination, and stood, gaping, in one spot. The front of the house was adorned with a small porch, its roof supported on two oak pillars—a welcome protection from the sun, which at that season in Little Russia [the Ukraine] loves not to jest, and bathes the pedestrian from head to foot in boiling perspiration. From this it may be judged how powerful was Ivan Ivanovich's desire to obtain an indispensable article, when he made up his mind, at such an hour, to depart from his usual custom, which was to walk about only in the evening.

The room which Ivan Ivanovich entered was quite dark, for the shutters were closed; and the ray of sunlight falling through a hole made in the shutter, took on the colors of the rainbow, and, striking the opposite wall, sketched upon it a party-colored picture of the outlines of roofs, trees, and the clothes suspended in the yard, only upside down. This gave the room a peculiar half-light.

"God assist you!" said Ivan Ivanovich.

"Ah! how do you do, Ivan Ivanovich?" replied a voice from the corner of the room. Then only did Ivan Ivanovich perceive Ivan Nikiforovich, lying upon a rug which was spread on the floor. "Excuse me for appearing before you in a state of nature."

"Not at all. You have been asleep to-day, Ivan Nikiforovich?"

"I have been asleep. Have you been asleep, Ivan Ivanovich?"

"I have."

"And now you have risen?"

"Now I have risen. Christ be with you, Ivan Nikiforovich! How can you sleep until this time? I have just come from the farm. There's very fine barley on the road, charming! and the hay is so tall and soft and golden!"

"Gorpina!" shouted Ivan Nikiforovich, "fetch Ivan Ivanovich some vodka, and some pastry and sour cream!"

"Fine weather, we're having to-day."

"Don't praise it, Ivan Ivanovich! Devil take it! You can't get away from the heat."

"Now, why need you mention the Devil! Ah, Ivan Nikiforovich! you will recall my words when it's too late. You will suffer in the next world for such godless words."

"How have I offended you, Ivan Ivanovich? I have not attacked your father nor your mother. I don't know how I have insulted you."

"Enough, enough, Ivan Nikiforovich!"

"By Heavens, Ivan Ivanovich, I did not insult you!"

"It's strange that the quails haven't come yet to the whistle."

"Think what you please, but I have not insulted you in any way."

"I don't know why they don't come," said Ivan Ivanovich, as if he did not hear Ivan Nikiforovich; "it is more than time for them already; . . . but they seem to need more time, for some reason."

"You say that the barley is good?"

"Splendid barley, splendid!"

A silence ensued.

"So you are having your clothes aired, Ivan Nikiforovich?" said Ivan Ivanovich, at length.

"Yes: those cursed women have ruined some beautiful clothes; almost new, they were, too. Now I'm having them aired: the cloth is fine and handsome. They only need turning to make them fit to wear again."

"One thing among them pleased me extremely, Ivan Nikiforovich."

"Which was that?"

"Tell me, please, what do you do with the gun that has been put to air with the clothes?" Here Ivan Ivanovich offered his snuff. "May I ask you to do me the favor?"

"By no means! take it yourself: I will use my own." Thereupon Ivan Nikiforovich felt about him, and got hold of his snuff-box. "That stupid woman! So she hung the gun out to air. That Jew makes good snuff in

Sorochintzi. I don't know what he puts into it, but it is so fragrant. It is a little like tansy. Here, take a little, and chew it: isn't it like tansy?"

"Say, Ivan Nikiforovich, I want to talk about that gun: what are you going to do with it? You don't need it."

"Why don't I need it? I might want to shoot."

"God be with you, Ivan Nikiforovich! When will you shoot? At the millennium, perhaps? So far as I know, or any one can recollect, you never killed even a duck: yes, and your nature was not so constructed that you can shoot. You have a dignified bearing and figure: how are you to drag yourself about the marshes, when your garment, which it is not polite to mention in conversation by name, is being aired at this very moment? What then? No: you require rest, repose." (Ivan Ivanovich, as has been hinted at above, employed uncommonly picturesque language when it was necessary to persuade any one. How he talked! Heavens, how he could talk!) "Yes, and you require polite actions. See here, give it to me!"

"The idea! The gun is valuable: you can't find such guns anywhere nowadays. I bought it of a Turk when I joined the militia; and now, to give it away all of a sudden! Impossible! It is an indispensable article."

"Indispensable for what?"

"For what? What if robbers should attack the house? . . . Indispensable indeed! Glory to God! now I am at ease, and fear no one. And why? Because I know that a gun stands in my store-house."

"A fine gun that! Why, Ivan Nikiforovich, the hammer is spoiled."

"What! how spoiled? It can be repaired: all that needs to be done is to rub it with hemp-oil, so that it may not rust."

"I see in your words, Ivan Nikiforovich, anything but a friendly disposition towards me. You will do nothing for me in token of friendship."

"How can you say, Ivan Ivanovich, that I show you no friendship? You ought to be ashamed of yourself. Your oxen pasture on my steppes, and I have never interfered with them. When you go to Poltava, you always beg my wagon, and what then? Have I ever refused? Your children climb over the fence into my yard, and play with my dogs—I never say anything; let them play, so long as they touch nothing; let them play!"

"If you won't give it to me, then let us exchange."

"What will you give me for it?" Thereupon Ivan Nikiforovich raised himself on his elbow, and looked at Ivan Ivanovich.

"I will give you my dark-brown sow, the one I have fed in the sty. A magnificent sow. You'll see, she'll bring you a litter of pigs next year."

"I do not see, Ivan Ivanovich, how you can talk so. What could I do with your sow? Make a funeral dinner for the Devil?"

"Again! You can't get along without the Devil! It's a sin! by Heaven, it's a sin, Ivan Nikiforovich!"

"What do you mean, in fact, Ivan Ivanovich, by giving, the deuce knows what—a sow—for my gun?"

"Why is she 'the deuce knows what,' Ivan Nikiforovich?"

"Why? You can judge for yourself perfectly well: here's the gun, a known thing; but the deuce knows what that sow is! If it had not been you who said it, Ivan Ivanovich, I might have put an insulting construction on it."

"What defect have you observed in the sow?"

"For what do you take me, in fact—for a sow?" . . .

"Sit down, sit down! I won't . . . No matter about your gun; let it rot and rust where it stands, in the corner of the storeroom. I don't want to say anything more about it!"

After this a pause ensued.

"They say," began Ivan Ivanovich, "that three kings have declared war on our Tzar."

"Yes: Peter Feodorovich told me. What sort of a war is this, and why?"

"I cannot say exactly, Ivan Nikiforovich, what the cause is. I suppose the kings want us to adopt the Turkish faith."

"Fools! they would have it," said Ivan Nikiforovich, raising his head.

"So, you see, our Tzar declared war on them in consequence. 'No,' says he, 'do you adopt the faith of Christ!' "

"What? Why, our people will beat them, Ivan Ivanovich!"

"They will. So you won't swap the gun, Ivan Nikiforovich?"

"It's a strange thing to me, Ivan Ivanovich, that you, who seem to be a man distinguished for sense, should talk such nonsense. What a fool I should be!"

"Sit down, sit down. God be with it! let it burst! I won't mention it again."

At this moment, lunch was brought in.

Ivan Ivanovich drank a glass, and ate a pie with sour cream. "Listen, Ivan Nikiforovich: I will give you, besides the sow, two sacks of oats; you did not sow any oats. You'll have to buy oats this year, in any case."

"By Heaven, Ivan Ivanovich, I must tell you, you are very green! [This is nothing: Ivan Nikiforovich does not even stop at such phrases.] Who ever heard of swapping a gun for two sacks of oats? Never fear, you don't offer your coat."

"But you forget, Ivan Nikiforovich, that I am to give you the sow too."

"What! two sacks of oats and a sow for a gun?"

"Why, is it too little?"

"For a gun?"

"Of course, for a gun."

"Two sacks for a gun?"

"Two sacks, not empty, but filled with oats; and you've forgotten the sow."

"Kiss your sow; and, if you don't like that, then go to the Evil One!"

"Oh, get angry now, do! See here: they'll stick your tongue full of red-hot needles in the other world, for such godless words. After a conversation with you, one has to wash his face and hands, and fumigate himself."

"Permit me, Ivan Ivanovich: my gun is a noble thing, the most curious toy; and, besides, it is a very agreeable decoration in a room.". . .

"You go on like a fool about that gun of yours, Ivan Nikiforovich," said Ivan Ivanovich with vexation; for he was beginning to be really angry.

"And you, Ivan Ivanovich, are a regular *goose!*"

If Ivan Nikiforovich had not uttered that word, then they would have quarrelled, but would have parted friends as usual; but now things took quite another turn. Ivan Ivanovich flew into a rage.

"What was that you said, Ivan Nikiforovich?" he asked, raising his voice.

"I said you were like a goose, Ivan Ivanovich!"

"How dare you, sir, forgetful of decency, and the respect due a man's rank and family, insult him with such a disgraceful name!"

"What is there disgraceful about it? And why are you flourishing your hands so, Ivan Ivanovich?"

"How dared you, I repeat, in disregard of all decency, call me a goose?"

"I spit on your head, Ivan Ivanovich! What are you screaming so for?"

Ivan Ivanovich could no longer control himself: his lips quivered; his mouth lost its usual V shape, and became like the letter O; he winked so that he was terrible to look at. This very rarely happened with Ivan Ivanovich: it was necessary that he should be extremely angry first.

"Then, I declare to you," exclaimed Ivan Ivanovich, "that I will not know you!"

"A great pity! By Heaven, I shall never cry on that account!" retorted Ivan Nikiforovich. He lied, he lied, by Heaven, he lied! it was very annoying to him.

"I will never put my foot inside your house again!"

"Oho, ho!" said Ivan Nikiforovich, vexed, yet not knowing himself what to do, and rising to his feet, contrary to his custom. "Hey, there, woman, boy!" Thereupon, there appeared at the door the same fat woman, and small boy, enveloped in a long and wide surtout. "Take Ivan Ivanovich by the arms, and lead him to the door!"

"What! a nobleman?" shouted Ivan Ivanovich with a feeling of vexation and dignity. "Just do it if you dare! Come on! I'll annihilate you and your stupid master. The crow won't be able to find your bones." (Ivan Ivanovich spoke with uncommon force when his spirit was up.)

The group presented a striking picture: Ivan Nikiforovich standing in the middle of the room; the woman with her mouth wide open, and the most senseless, terrified look on her face; Ivan Ivanovich with uplifted hand, as the Roman tribunes are depicted. This was an extraordinary moment, a magnificent spectacle: and yet there was but one spectator; this was the boy in the extensive surtout, who stood quite quietly, and picked his nose with his finger.

Finally Ivan Ivanovich took his hat. "You have behaved well, Ivan Nikiforovich, extremely well! I shall remember it."

"Go, Ivan Ivanovich, go! and see that you don't come in my way: if you do, I'll beat your ugly face to a jelly, Ivan Ivanovich!"

"Take that, Ivan Nikiforovich!" retorted Ivan Ivanovich, making an insulting gesture, and banged the door, which squeaked and flew open behind him.

Ivan Nikiforovich appeared at the door, and wanted to add something more; but Ivan Ivanovich did not glance back, and hastened from the yard.

III.

What Took Place after Ivan Ivanovich's Quarrel with Ivan Nikiforovich.

AND THUS TWO respectable men, the pride and honor of Mirgorod, had quarrelled, and about what? About a bit of nonsense—a goose. They would not see each other, broke off all connection, while hitherto they had been known as the most inseparable friends. Every day Ivan Ivanovich and Ivan Nikiforovich had sent to inquire about each other's health, and often conversed together from their balconies, and said such charming things as it did the heart good to listen to. On Sundays, Ivan Ivanovich, in his lambskin bekesha, and Ivan Nikiforovich, in his yellowish cinnamon-colored nankeen casaquin, used to set out for church almost arm in arm; and if Ivan Ivanovich, who had remarkably sharp eyes, was the first to catch sight of a puddle or any dirt in the street, which sometimes happened in Mirgorod, he always said to Ivan Nikiforovich, "Look out! don't put your foot there, it's dirty." Ivan Nikiforovich, on his side, exhibited the same touching tokens of friendship; and wherever he chanced to be standing, he always held out his hand to Ivan Ivanovich with his snuff-box, saying, "Do me the favor!" And what fine managers both were. . . . And these two friends . . . When I heard of it, it struck me like a flash of lightning. For a long time I would not believe it. Ivan Ivanovich had quarrelled with Ivan Nikiforovich! Such worthy people! What is to be depended upon, then, in this world?

When Ivan Ivanovich reached home, he remained long in a state of strong excitement. He usually went, first of all, to the stable, to see whether his mare was eating her hay (Ivan Ivanovich had a bay mare, with a white star on her forehead: a very pretty little mare she was too), then to feed the turkeys and little pigs with his own hand, and then to his room, where he either made wooden dishes (he could make various vessels of wood very tastefully, quite as well as any turner), or read a book printed by Liubia, Garia and Popoff (Ivan Ivanovich never could remember the name, because the serving-maid had long before torn off the top part of the title page while amusing the children), or rested on the veranda. But now he did not betake himself to any of his ordinary occupations. Instead, on encountering Gapka, he began to scold because she was loitering about without any occupation, though she was carrying groats to the kitchen; flung a stick at a cock which came upon the veranda for his customary treat; and when the dirty little boy, in his little torn blouse, ran up to him, and shouted, "Papa, papa! give me a honey-cake," he threatened him and stamped at him so fiercely that the frightened child fled, God knows whither.

But at last he bethought himself, and began to busy himself with his every-day duties. He dined late, and it was almost night when he lay down to rest on the veranda. A good beet-soup with pigeons, which Gapka cooked for him, quite drove from his mind the occurrences of the morning. Again Ivan Ivanovich began to gaze at his belongings with satisfaction: at length his eye rested on the neighboring yard; and he said to himself, "I have not been to Ivan Nikiforovich's to-day: I'll go there now." So saying, Ivan Ivanovich took his stick and his hat, and directed his steps to the street; but scarcely had he passed through the gate, when he recollected the quarrel, spit, and turned back. Almost the same thing happened at Ivan Nikiforovich's house. Ivan Ivanovich saw the woman put her foot on the fence, with the intention of climbing over into his yard, when suddenly Ivan Nikiforovich's voice became audible. "Back! back! it won't do!" But Ivan Ivanovich found it very tiresome. It is quite possible that these worthy men would have made peace next day, if a certain occurrence in Ivan Ivanovich's house had not destroyed all hopes, and poured oil upon the fire of enmity which was ready to die out.

.   .   .   .   .   .

On the evening of that very day, Agafya Fedosyevna arrived at Ivan Nikiforovich's. Agafya Fedosyevna was not Ivan Nikiforovich's relative, nor his sister-in-law, nor even his fellow-godparent. There seemed to be no reason why she should come to him, and he was not particularly glad of her company; still, she came, and lived on him for weeks at a time, and even longer. Then she took possession of the keys, and took the whole house into her own hands. This was extremely displeasing to Ivan

Nikiforovich; but he, to his amazement, minded her like a child; and although he occasionally attempted to dispute, yet Agafya Fedosyevna always got the better of him.

I must confess that I do not understand why things are so arranged, that women seize us by the nose as deftly as they do the handle of a teapot: either their hands are so constructed, or else our noses are good for nothing else. And notwithstanding the fact that Ivan Nikiforovich's nose somewhat resembled a plum, she grasped that nose, and led him about after her like a dog. He even, in her presence, involuntarily altered his ordinary manner of life.

Agafya Fedosyevna wore a cap on her head, three warts on her nose, and a coffee-colored cloak with yellow flowers. Her figure was like a cask, and it would have been as hard to tell where to look for her waist, as for her to see her nose without a mirror. Her feet were small, and formed in the shape of two cushions. She talked scandal, and ate boiled beet-soup in the morning, and swore extremely well; and amidst all these various occupations, her countenance never for one instant changed its expression, which phenomenon, as a rule, women alone are capable of displaying.

Just as soon as she arrived, everything went wrong side before. "Ivan Nikiforovich, don't you make peace with him, nor ask his forgiveness; he wants to ruin you; that's the kind of man he is! you don't know him yet!" that cursed woman whispered and whispered, and managed so that Ivan Nikiforovich would not even hear Ivan Ivanovich mentioned.

All assumed another aspect. If his neighbor's dog ran into the yard, it was beaten within an inch of its life; the children, who climbed over the fence, were sent back with howls, their little shirts stripped up, and marks of a switch behind; even the woman, when Ivan Ivanovich undertook to ask her about something, did something so insulting, that Ivan Ivanovich, being an extremely delicate man, only spit, and muttered, "What a nasty woman! even worse than her master!"

Finally, as a climax to all the insults, his hated neighbor built a goose-coop right against his fence where they usually climbed over, as if with the express intention of redoubling the insult. This coop, so hateful to Ivan Ivanovich, was constructed with diabolical swiftness—in one day.

This aroused wrath and a desire for revenge in Ivan Ivanovich. Nevertheless, he showed no signs of bitterness, in spite of the fact that the coop trespassed on his land; but his heart beat so violently, that it was extremely difficult for him to preserve this calm appearance.

He passed through the day in this manner. Night came. . . . Oh, if I were a painter, how magnificently I would depict the night's charms! I would describe how all Mirgorod sleeps; how steadily the myriads of stars gaze down upon it; how the apparent quiet is filled far and near with the barking of dogs; how the love-sick sacristan steals past them, and scales the fence with knightly fearlessness; how the white walls of the houses, bathed in the moonlight, grow whiter still, the overhanging trees darker; how the shadows of the trees fall blacker, the flowers and the silent grass become more fragrant, and the crickets, unharmonious cavaliers of the night, strike up their rattling song in friendly fashion on all sides. I would describe how, in one of these little, low-roofed, clay houses, the black-browed village maid, tossing on her lonely couch, dreams with heaving bosom of hussar's spurs and mustache, and how the moonlight smiles upon her cheeks. I would describe how the black shadows of the bats flit along the white road, before they alight upon the white chimneys of the cottages. . . .

But it would hardly be within my power to depict Ivan Ivanovich, as he crept out that night, saw in hand; and the various emotions written on his countenance! Quietly, so quietly, he crawled along, and climbed upon the goose-coop. Ivan Nikiforovich's dogs knew nothing, as yet, of the quarrel between them; and so they permitted him, as an old friend, to enter the coop, which rested upon four oaken posts. Creeping up to the nearest post, he applied his saw, and began to cut. The noise produced by the saw caused him to glance about him every moment, but the recollection of the insult refreshed his courage. The first post was sawed through. Ivan Ivanovich began upon the next. His eyes burned, and he saw nothing for terror. All at once Ivan Ivanovich uttered an exclamation, and became petrified with fear: a dead man appeared to him; but he speedily recovered himself on perceiving that it was a goose, thrusting its neck out at him. Ivan Ivanovich spit with vexation, and proceeded with his work; and the second post was sawed through. The building trembled. Ivan Ivanovich's heart beat so violently, when he began on the third, that he had to stop several times. The post was more than half sawed through, when the frail building quivered violently. . . .

Ivan Ivanovich had barely time to spring back when it tumbled down with a crash. Seizing his saw, he ran home in the greatest terror, and flung himself upon his bed, without having sufficient courage to peep from the window at the consequences of his terrible deed. It seemed to him as though Ivan Nikiforovich's entire household assembled: the old woman, Ivan Nikiforovich, the boy in the endless surtout, all with sticks, . . . led by Agafya Fedosyevna, were coming to tear down and destroy his house.

Ivan Ivanovich passed the whole of the following day in a perfect fever. It seemed to him that his detested neighbor would set fire to his house at least, in revenge for this; and so he gave orders to Gapka to look everywhere constantly, and see whether dry straw were laid against it anywhere. Finally, in order to forestall Ivan Nikiforovich, he determined to run ahead, like a hare, and enter a complaint against him before the district judge of Mirgorod. In what it consisted, can be learned from the following chapter.

IV.

What Took Place before the District Judge of Mirgorod.

A WONDERFUL TOWN is Mirgorod! How many buildings are there under straw, rush, and even wooden roofs! On the right is a street, on the left a street, and fine fences everywhere: over them twine hop-vines, upon them hang pots; from behind them the sunflowers show their sun-like heads, poppies blush, fat pumpkins peep, . . . luxury itself! The fence is always garnished with articles which render it still more picturesque: women's widespread undergarments of checked woollen stuff, shirts or trousers. There is no such thing as theft or rascality in Mirgorod, so everybody hangs upon his fence whatever strikes his fancy. If you will go to the square, you will surely stop and admire the view: a puddle, such a wonderful puddle, is there! the only one you ever saw. It occupies nearly the whole of the square. A truly magnificent puddle! The houses and cottages, which at a distance might be mistaken for hay-ricks, stand around it, lost in admiration of its beauty.

But I agree with those who think that there is no better house than that of the district judge. Whether it is of oak or birch, is nothing to the point; but it has, my dear sirs, eight windows! eight windows in a row, directly on the square, and upon that watery expanse, which I have just mentioned, and which the chief of police calls a lake. It alone is painted the color of granite. All the other houses in Mirgorod are merely whitewashed. Its roof is all of wood, and would have been even painted red, had not the government clerks eaten the oil which had been prepared for that purpose, having flavored it with garlic, as it happened, as if expressly, during a fast; and so the roof remained unpainted. Towards the square projects a porch, which the chickens frequently visit, because that porch is nearly always strewn with grain or some edible, not intentionally, but through the carelessness of visitors. The house is divided into two parts: one part is the court-room; the other, the jail. In the half which contains the court-room are two neat, whitewashed rooms—one, the front one, for clients, the other containing a table adorned with ink-spots. Upon the table is a looking-glass; there are four oak chairs with tall backs; along the wall stand iron-bound chests, in which are preserved bundles of district law-suit papers. Upon one of the chests stood at that time a pair of boots, polished with wax.

The court had been open since morning. The judge, a pretty large man, though thinner than Ivan Nikiforovich, with a good-natured face, a greasy dressing-gown, a pipe, and a cup of tea, was conversing with the clerk of the court.

The judge's lips were directly under his nose, so that he could snuff his upper lip as much as he liked. This lip served him instead of a snuff-box, for the snuff intended for his nose almost always lodged upon it. So the judge was talking with the assistant. A barefooted girl held a tray with cups on one side of them. At the end of the table, the secretary was reading the decision in some case, but in such a mournful and monotonous voice, that the condemned man himself would have fallen asleep while listening to it. The judge, no doubt, would have been the first of all to do so, had he not entered into an engrossing conversation while it was going on.

"I expressly tried to find out," said the judge, sipping his tea from the already cold cup, "how they manage to sing so well. I had a splendid thrush two years ago. Well, all of a sudden he was completely spoiled, and began to sing God knows what: he got worse, and worse, and worse, as time went on; he began to rattle and get hoarse—just good for nothing! And it's all nonsense! this is why it happened: a little lump, not so big as a pea, came under his throat. It was only necessary to prick that little swelling with a needle. Zachar Prokofievich taught me that; and, if you like, I'll tell you just how it was. I go to him" . . .

"Shall I read another, Demyan Demyanovich?" broke in the secretary, who had not been reading for several minutes.

"Have you finished already? Just think how quick! And I did not hear a word of it! Where is it? Give it here, and I'll sign it. What else have you there?"

"The case of Cossack Bokítok for stealing a cow."

"Very good; read it! Yes, so I go to him. . . . I can even tell you in detail how he entertained me. There was vodka and dried sturgeon, excellent! Yes, not our sturgeon" (here the judge smacked his tongue, and smiled, upon which his nose took a snuff at its usual snuff-box), "such as our Mirgorod shops furnish us. I ate no herrings, for, as you know, they give me heart-burn; but I tasted the caviare—very fine caviare! There's no doubt about it, excellent. Then I drank some peach-brandy, real gentian. There was saffron-brandy too; but, as you know, I never take that. You see, it was very good. In the first place, to whet your appetite, as they say, and then to satisfy it . . . Ah! speak of an angel" . . . exclaimed the judge, all at once, catching sight of Ivan Ivanovich as he entered.

"God be with us! I wish you a good-morning," said Ivan Ivanovich, bowing all round with his usual politeness. My God! how well he understood the art of fascinating everybody with all his ways! I never beheld such refinement. He knew his own worth quite well, and therefore looked for universal respect as his due. The judge himself handed Ivan Ivanovich a chair; and his nose inhaled all the snuff from his upper lip, which, with him, was always a sign of great pleasure.

"What will you take, Ivan Ivanovich?" he inquired: "will you have a cup of tea?"

"No, much obliged," replied Ivan Ivanovich, bowed and seated himself.

"Do me the favor—one little cup," repeated the judge.

"No, thank you; much obliged for your hospitality," replied Ivan Ivanovich, and rose, bowed, and sat down.

"Just one little cup," repeated the judge.

"No, do not trouble yourself, Demyan Demyanovich." Whereupon Ivan Ivanovich again rose, bowed, and sat down.

"A little cup!"

"Very well, then, just a little cup," said Ivan Ivanovich, and reached out his hand to the tray.

My Heavens! What a depth of refinement there was in that man! It is impossible to describe what a pleasant impression such manners produce!

"Will you not have another cup?"

"I thank you sincerely," answered Ivan Ivanovich, turning his cup upside down upon the tray, and bowing.

"Do me the favor, Ivan Ivanovich."

"I cannot; much obliged." Thereupon Ivan Ivanovich bowed, and sat down.

"Ivan Ivanovich, for the sake of our friendship, just one little cup!"

"No: I am extremely indebted for your hospitality." So saying, Ivan Ivanovich bowed, and seated himself.

"Only a cup, one little cup!"

Ivan Ivanovich put out his hand to the tray, and took a cup.

Oh, the deuce! How, how can a man contrive to support his dignity!

"Demyan Demyanovich," said Ivan Ivanovich, swallowing the last mouthful, "I have pressing business with you: I want to enter a complaint."

Then Ivan Ivanovich set down his cup, and drew from his pocket a sheet of stamped paper, written over. "A complaint against my enemy, my sworn enemy."

"And who is that?"

"Ivan Nikiforovich Dovgochkhun."

At these words, the judge nearly fell off his chair. "What do you say?" he exclaimed, clasping his hands: "Ivan Ivanovich, is this you?"

"You see yourself, that it is I."

"The Lord and all the saints be with you! What! You! Ivan Ivanovich! you have fallen out with Ivan Nikiforovich! Is it your mouth which says that? Repeat it! Is not some one hid behind you, who is speaking instead of you?"

"What is there incredible about it? I can't endure the sight of him: he has done me a deadly injury—he has insulted my honor."

"Holy Trinity! How am I to believe my mother now? Why, every day, when I quarrel with my sister, the old woman says, 'Children, you live together like dogs. If you would only take pattern by Ivan Ivanovich and Ivan Nikiforovich, they are friends indeed! such friends! such worthy people!' There you are with your friend! Tell me what this is about. How is it?"

"It is a delicate business, Demyan Demyanovich; it is impossible to relate it in words: be pleased rather to read my petition. Here, take it by this side: it is more convenient."

"Read it, Taras Tikhonovich," said the judge, turning to the secretary. Taras Tikhonovich took the petition; and blowing his nose, as all district judges' secretaries blow their noses, with the assistance of two fingers, he began to read:

"From the nobleman and landed proprietor of the Mirgorod District, Ivan Pererépenko, son of Ivan, a petition: concerning which the following points are to be observed:

"1. Ivan Dovgochkhun, son of Nikifor, nobleman, known to all the world for his godless acts, which inspire disgust, and in lawlessness exceed all bounds, on the seventh day of July of this year 1810, conferred upon me a deadly insult, as touching my personal honor, and likewise as tending to the humiliation and confusion of my rank and family. The said nobleman, of repulsive aspect, has also a pugnacious disposition, and is full to overflowing of various sorts of blasphemy and quarrelsome words.". . .

Here the reader paused for an instant, to blow his nose again; but the judge folded his hands in approbation, and murmured to himself, "What a ready pen! Lord! how that man does write!"

Ivan Ivanovich requested that the reading might proceed, and Taras Tikhonovich went on:

"The said Ivan Dovgochkhun, son of Nikifor, when I went to him with a friendly proposition, called me publicly by an epithet insulting and injurious to my honor, namely, a *goose*, whereas it is known to the whole district of Mirgorod, that I never was named after that disgusting animal, and have no intention of ever being named after it. And the proof of my noble extraction is, that, in the baptismal register to be found in the Church of the Three Bishops, the day of my birth, and likewise the fact of my baptism, are inscribed. But a goose, as is well known to every one who has any knowledge of science, cannot be inscribed in the baptismal register; for a goose is not a man, but a fowl; which, likewise, is sufficiently well known, even to persons who have not been to a seminary. But the said evil-minded nobleman, being privy to all these facts, for no other purpose than to offer a deadly insult to my rank and calling, affronted me with the aforesaid foul word.

"2. And the same impolite and indecent nobleman, moreover, attempted injury to my property, inherited by me from my father, a member of the clerical profession, Ivan Pererépenko, son of Onisieff, of blessed memory, in that he, contrary to all law, transported directly opposite my porch, a goose-coop, which was done with no other intention than to emphasize the insult offered me; for the said coop had, up to that time, stood in a very good situation, and was still sufficiently strong. But the loathsome intention of the aforesaid nobleman consisted simply in this: viz., in making me a witness of unpleasant occurrences; for it is well known, that no man goes into a coop, much less into a goose-coop, for polite purposes. In the commission of his lawless deed, the two front posts trespassed on my land, received by me during the lifetime of my father, Ivan Pererépenko, son of Onisieff, of blessed memory, beginning at the granary, thence in a straight line to the spot where the women wash the pots.

"3. The above-described nobleman, whose very name and surname inspire thorough disgust, cherishes in his mind a malicious design to burn me in my own house. Which the infallible signs, hereinafter mentioned, fully demonstrate: in the first place, the said wicked nobleman has begun to emerge frequently from his apartments, which he never did formerly on account of his laziness and the disgusting corpulence of his body; in the second place, in his servants' apartments, adjoining the fence, surrounding my own land, received by me from my father, of blessed memory, Ivan Pererépenko, son of Onisieff, a light burns every day, and for a remarkably long period of time, which is also a clear proof of the fact. For hitherto, owing to his repulsive niggardliness, not only the tallow-candle, but also the grease-lamp, has been extinguished.

"And therefore I pray that the said nobleman, Ivan Dovgochkhun, son of Ivan, being plainly guilty of incendiarism, of insult to my rank, name, and family, and of illegal appropriation of my property, and, worse than all else, of malicious and deliberate addition to my surname, of the nickname of goose, be condemned by the court, to fine, satisfaction, costs, and damages, and that the aforesaid be put in irons as a criminal, and, being chained, be removed to the town jail, and that judgment be rendered upon this, my petition, immediately and without delay.

"Written and composed by Ivan Pererépenko, son of Ivan, nobleman, and landed proprietor of Mirgorod."

After the reading of the petition was concluded, the judge approached Ivan Ivanovich, took him by the button, and began to talk to him after this fashion. "What are you doing, Ivan Ivanovich? Fear God! throw away that petition, let it go! may Satan carry it off! Better take Ivan Nikiforovich by the hand, and kiss him, and buy some Santurinski or Nikopolski liquor, simply make a punch, and call me. We will drink it up together, and forget all."

"No, Demyan Demyanovich! it's not that sort of an affair," said Ivan Ivanovich, with the dignity which always became him so well; "it is not an affair which can be arranged by a friendly agreement. Farewell! Good-day to you also, gentlemen," he continued with the same dignity, turning to them all. "I hope that my petition will give rise to the proper action." And out he went, leaving all present in a state of stupefaction.

The judge sat down without uttering a word; the secretary took a pinch of snuff; the clerks upset some broken fragments of bottles which served for ink-stands; and the judge himself, in absence of mind, spread out a puddle of ink upon the table with his finger.

"What do you say to this, Dorofei Trofimovich?" said the judge, turning to the assistant after a pause.

"I've nothing to say," replied the clerk.

"What things do go on!" continued the judge. He had not finished saying this, when the door creaked, and the front half of Ivan Nikiforovich presented itself in the court-room: the rest of him remained in the ante-room. The appearance of Ivan Nikiforovich, and in court, too, seemed so extraordinary, that the judge screamed; the secretary stopped reading; and one clerk, in his frieze imitation of a dress-coat, took his pen in his lips; and the other swallowed a fly; even the constable on service, and the watchman, a discharged soldier, who up to that moment had stood by the door scratching about his dirty blouse, with its chevrons of merit on the shoulder, even this invalid dropped his jaw, and trod on some one's foot.

"What chance brings you here? What and how? How is your health, Ivan Nikiforovich?"

But Ivan Nikiforovich was neither dead nor alive; for he was stuck fast in the door, and could not take a step either forwards or backwards. In vain did the judge shout into the ante-room that some one there should push Ivan Nikiforovich forward into the court-room. In the ante-room was only one old woman with a petition, who, in spite of all the efforts of her bony hands, could accomplish nothing. Then one of the clerks, with thick lips, wide shoulders, and a thick nose, with eyes which looked askance and intoxicated, and with ragged elbows, approached the front half of Ivan Nikiforovich, crossed his hands for him as though he had been a child, and winked at the old soldier, who braced his knee against Ivan Nikiforovich's belly. In spite of the latter's piteous moans, he was squeezed out into the ante-room. Then they pulled the bolts, and opened the other half of the door. Meanwhile the clerk and his assistant, the soldier, breathing hard with their friendly exertions, exhaled such a strong odor that the court-room seemed temporarily converted into a drinking-room.

"Did you hurt yourself, Ivan Nikiforovich? I will tell my mother to send you a decoction of brandy, with which you need but to rub your back and stomach, and all your bad feelings will disappear."

But Ivan Nikiforovich dropped into a chair, and could utter no word beyond prolonged *oh's*. Finally, in a voice feeble and barely audible from fatigue, he exclaimed, "Wouldn't you like some?" and, drawing his snuff-box from his pocket, he added, "Help yourself, if you please."

"Very glad to see you," replied the judge; "but I cannot conceive what made you put yourself to so much trouble, and favor us with so unexpected an honor."

"A petition!" . . . Ivan Nikiforovich managed to ejaculate.

"A petition? What petition?"

"A complaint" . . . (here the asthma entailed a prolonged pause)— "Oh!—a complaint against the rascal—Ivan Ivanovich Pererépenko!"

"And you too! Such particular friends! A complaint against such a benevolent man!"

"He's Satan himself!" ejaculated Ivan Nikiforovich abruptly.

The judge crossed himself.

"Take my petition, and read it."

"There is nothing to be done. Read it, Taras Tikhonovich," said the judge, turning to the secretary with an expression of displeasure, which caused his nose to sniff at his upper lip, which generally occurred only as a sign of great enjoyment. This independence on the part of his nose caused the judge still greater vexation. He pulled out his handkerchief, and rubbed off all the snuff from his upper lip, in order to punish it for its daring.

The secretary, having gone through his usual performance, which he always indulged in before he began to read—that is to say, without the aid of a pocket-handkerchief—began in his ordinary voice, in the following manner:

"Ivan Dovgochkhun, son of Nikofor, nobleman of the Mirgorod District, offers a petition, and begs attention to the following points:

"1. Through his hateful malice, and plainly manifested ill will, the person calling himself a nobleman, Ivan Pererépenko, son of Ivan, commits against me every manner of injury, damage, and other spiteful deeds, which inspire me with terror; and yesterday at afternoon, like a brigand and a thief, with axes, saws, chisels, and various locksmith's tools, he came by night into my yard, and into my own goose-coop located within it, and with his own hand, and in outrageous manner, destroyed it; for which very illegal and burglarious deed, on my side I gave no manner of cause.

"2. The same nobleman Pererépenko has designs upon my life; and on the 7th of last month, cherishing this design in secret, he came to me, and began, in a friendly and sly manner, to demand of me a gun which was in my chamber, and offered me for it, with the miserliness peculiar to him, many worthless objects, such as a brown sow and two sacks of oats. But, divining at that time his criminal intentions, I endeavored in every way to dissuade him from it; but the said rascal and scoundrel, Ivan Pererépenko, son of Ivan, abused me like a muzhik, and since that time has cherished against me an irreconcilable enmity. His sister was well known to all the world as a loose character, and went off with a regiment of chasseurs which was stationed at Mirgorod, five years ago; but she inscribed her husband as a peasant. His father and mother also were not law-abiding people, and both were inconceivable drunkards. The afore-mentioned nobleman and robber Pererépenko, in his beastly and blame-worthy actions, goes beyond all his family, and under the guise of piety does the most immoral things. He does not observe the fasts; for on the eve of St. Philip's this atheist bought a sheep, and the next day he ordered his mistress, Gapka, to kill it, alleging that he needed tallow for lamps and candles at once.

"Therefore I pray that the said nobleman, a manifest robber, church-thief, rascal, convicted of plundering and stealing, may be put in irons, and confined in the jail or the government prison, and there, under supervision, deprived of his rank and nobility, he may be well flogged by barbarians, and banished to forced labor in Siberia for cause, and that he may be commanded to pay damages, losses, and that judgment may be rendered on this my petition.

"To this petition, Ivan Dovgochkhun, son of Nikofor, noble of the Mirgorod District, has set his hand."

As soon as the secretary had finished reading, Ivan Nikiforovich seized his hat, and bowed, with the intention of departing.

"Where are you going, Ivan Nikiforovich?" the judge called after him. "Sit yet a little while. Drink some tea. Orishko, why are you standing there, you stupid girl, winking at the clerks? Go, bring tea."

But Ivan Nikiforovich, in terror at having got so far from home, and at having undergone such a fearful quarantine, made haste to crawl through the door, saying, "Don't trouble yourself. It is with pleasure that I"—and closed it after him, leaving all present stupefied.

There was nothing to be done. Both petitions were entered; and the affair promised to assume a sufficiently serious aspect, when an unforeseen occurrence gave an added interest to it. As the judge was leaving the court, in company with the clerk and secretary, and the employees were thrusting into sacks the fowls, eggs, chunks of bread, pies, cracknels, and other odds and ends brought by plaintiffs—just at that moment a brown sow rushed into the room, and snatched, to the amazement of the spectators, neither a pie nor a crust of bread, but Ivan Nikiforovich's petition, which lay on the end of the table, with its leaves hanging over. Having seized the document, mistress sow ran off so briskly that not one of the clerks or officials could catch her, in spite of the rulers and inkbottles they hurled after her.

This extraordinary occurrence produced a terrible muddle, for there had not even a copy been taken of the petition. The judge—that is to say, his secretary—and the assistant debated for a long time upon such an unheard-of affair. Finally it was decided to write a report of the matter to the prefect, as the investigation of the matter pertained more to the department of the city police. Report No. 389 was despatched to him that same day; and also upon that day there came to light a sufficiently curious explanation, which the reader can learn from the following chapter.

V.

IN WHICH ARE DETAILED THE DELIBERATIONS OF TWO IMPORTANT PERSONAGES OF MIRGOROD.

As SOON AS Ivan Ivanovich had arranged his domestic affairs, and stepped out upon the veranda, according to his custom, to lie down, then, to his indescribable amazement, he saw something red at the gate. This was the red facings of the chief of police's coat, which were polished equally with his collar, and had turned on the edges into varnished leather. Ivan Ivanovich thought to himself, "It's not bad that Peter Feodorovich has come to talk it over." But he was very much surprised to see that the chief was walking remarkably fast, and flourishing his hands, which very rarely happened with him. There were eight buttons planted about on the chief of police's uniform; the ninth, torn off in some manner during the procession at the consecration of the church two years before, the *desyatskie* [constables] had not been able to find up to this time; although the chief, on the occasion of the daily reports made to him by the sergeants of police, always asked, "Has that button been found?" These eight buttons were strewn about him as women sow beans—one to the right, and one to the left. His left foot had been struck by a ball in the last campaign, and therefore he limped, and threw it out so far to one side as to almost counteract the efforts of the right foot. The more briskly the chief of police worked his walking apparatus, the less progress it made in advance; and so, while the chief was getting to the veranda, Ivan Ivanovich had plenty of time to lose himself in surmises as to why the chief was flourishing his hands so vigorously. This interested him the more, as the matter seemed one of unusual importance; for the chief had on a new dagger.

"Good-morning, Peter Feodorovich!" cried Ivan Ivanovich, who was, as has already been stated, exceedingly curious, and could not restrain his impatience at the sight as the chief of police began to ascend to the veranda, yet never raised his eyes, and scolded at his foot, which could not be persuaded to mount the step at only one flourish.

"I wish my good friend and benefactor, Ivan Ivanovich, a good-day," replied the chief.

"Pray sit down. I see that you are weary, as your lame foot hinders" . . .

"My foot!" screamed the chief, bestowing upon Ivan Ivanovich a glance such as a giant might cast upon a pygmy, a pedant upon a dancing-master: thereupon he stretched out his foot, and stamped upon the floor with it. But this boldness cost him dear; for his whole body wavered, and his nose struck the railing; but the brave preserver of order, with the purpose of making light of it, righted himself immediately, and began to feel in his pocket as if to get his snuff-box. "I must report to you, my dear friend and benefactor, Ivan Ivanovich, that never in all my days have I made such a march. Yes, seriously. For instance, during the campaign of 1807. . . . Ah! I will relate to you in what manner I crawled through the enclosure to see a pretty little German." Here the chief closed one eye, and executed a diabolically sly smile.

"Where have you been to-day?" asked Ivan Ivanovich, wishing to cut the chief short, and bring him more speedily to the object of his visit. He would have very much liked to inquire what the chief meant to tell him, but his extensive knowledge of the world showed him all the impropriety of such a question; and so Ivan Ivanovich had to keep himself well in hand, and await a solution, his heart, meanwhile, beating with unusual force.

"Ah, excuse me! I was going to tell you—where was I?" answered the chief of police. "In the first place, I report that the weather is fine to-day" . . .

At these last words, Ivan Ivanovich nearly died.

"But permit me," went on the chief. "I came to you to-day about a very important affair." Here the chief's face and bearing assumed the same careworn guise with which he had ascended to the veranda. Ivan

Ivanovich lived again, and shook as if in a fever, omitting not, as was his habit, to put a question. "What is the important matter? Is it important?"

"Pray judge for yourself: first I venture to report to you, dear friend and benefactor, Ivan Ivanovich, that you . . . I beg you to observe that, for my own part, I should have nothing to say; but the rules of government require it . . . you have transgressed the rules of propriety."

"What do you say, Peter Feodorovich? I don't understand at all."

"Pardon me, Ivan Ivanovich! how is it that you do not understand? Your own beast has destroyed a very important government document; and you can still say, after that, that you do not understand!"

"What beast?"

"Your own brown sow, with your permission, be it said."

"How am I responsible? Why did the janitor of the court open the door?"

"But, Ivan Ivanovich, your own brown sow. You must be responsible."

"I am extremely obliged to you for comparing me to a sow."

"But I did not say that, Ivan Ivanovich! By Heavens! I did not say it! Pray judge from your own clear conscience. It is known to you without doubt, that, in accordance with the views of the government, unclean animals are forbidden to roam about the city, particularly in the principal streets. Confess, now, that it is prohibited."

"God knows what you are talking about! A mighty important business, that a sow got into the street!"

"Permit me to inform you, Ivan Ivanovich, permit me, permit me, that this is utterly impossible. What is to be done? The authorities command, we must obey. I don't deny, that sometimes chickens and geese run about the streets, and even about the square—pray observe, chickens and geese; but only last year, I gave orders that pigs and goats were not to be admitted to the public squares, which regulations I directed to be read aloud at the time, in the assembly before all the people."

"No, Peter Feodorovich, I see nothing here except that you are doing your best to insult me."

"But you cannot say, my dearest friend and benefactor, that I have tried to insult you. Bethink yourself: I never said a word to you last year when you built a roof a whole arshin higher than was fixed by law. On the contrary, I pretended not to have observed it. Believe me, my dearest friend, even now, I would, so to speak . . . but my duty, in a word, my obligations, demand that I should have an eye to cleanliness. Just judge for yourself, when suddenly in the principal street" . . .

"Fine principal streets yours are! Every woman goes there and throws down any rubbish she chooses."

"Permit me to inform you, Ivan Ivanovich, that it is you who are insulting me. In fact, that does sometimes happen, but, as a rule, only beside fences, sheds, or store-houses; but that a filthy sow should intrude herself in the main street, in the square, now that's a matter" . . .

"What sort of a matter? Peter Feodorovich! surely a sow is one of God's creatures!"

"Agreed. Everybody knows that you are a learned man, that you are acquainted with sciences and various other subjects. In short, I never studied the sciences: I began to learn to write in my thirteenth year. Of course you know that I was a soldier in the ranks."

"Hm!" said Ivan Ivanovich.

"Yes," continued the chief of police, "in 1801 I was in the Forty-second Regiment of chasseurs, lieutenant in the Fourth Battalion. The commander of our battalion was, if I may be permitted to mention it, Capt. Eremeeff." Thereupon the chief of police thrust his fingers into the snuff-box which Ivan Ivanovich was holding open, and stirred up the snuff.

Ivan Ivanovich answered, "Hm!"

"But my duty," went on the chief of police, "is to obey the commands of the authorities. Do you know, Ivan Ivanovich, that a person who purloins a government document in the court-room incurs capital punishment, equally with other criminals?"

"I know it; and, if you like, I can give you lessons. It is so ordered with regard to people—as if you, for instance, were to steal a document; but a sow is an animal, one of God's creatures."

"Certainly; but the law reads, 'Those guilty of theft' . . . I beg you to listen most attentively—'*Those guilty!*' Here is indicated neither race nor sex nor rank: of course, an animal can be guilty. You may say what you please; but the animal, until the sentence is pronounced by the court, should be committed to the charge of the police, as a transgressor of the law."

"No, Peter Feodorovich," retorted Ivan Ivanovich coolly, "that shall not be."

"As you like: only I must carry out the orders of the authorities."

"What are you threatening me with? Probably you want to send that one-armed soldier after her. I shall order the woman who tends the door to drive him off with the poker: he'll get his last arm broken."

"I dare not dispute with you. In case you will not commit her to the charge of the police, then do what you please with her: kill her for Christmas, if you like, and make hams of her, or eat her as she is. Only I should like to ask you, in case you make sausages, to send me a couple, such as your Gapka makes so well of blood and lard. My Agrafena Trofimovna is extremely fond of them."

"I will send you a couple of sausages if you permit."

"I shall be extremely obliged to you, dear friend and benefactor. Now permit me to say one word more. I am commissioned by the judge, as well as by all our acquaintances, so to speak, to effect a reconciliation between you and your friend, Ivan Nikiforovich."

"What! with that brute! I am to be reconciled to that clown! Never! It shall not be, it shall not be!" Ivan Ivanovich was in a remarkably determined frame of mind.

"As you like," replied the chief of police, treating both nostrils to snuff. "I will not venture to advise you; but permit me to mention—here you live at enmity, and if you make peace" . . .

But Ivan Ivanovich began to talk about catching quail, as he usually did when he wanted to put an end to a conversation. So the chief of police was obliged to retire without having achieved any success whatever.

VI.

FROM WHICH THE READER CAN EASILY DISCOVER WHAT IS CONTAINED IN IT.

IN SPITE of all the judge's efforts to keep the matter secret, all Mirgorod knew by the next day that Ivan Ivanovich's sow had stolen Ivan Nikiforovich's petition. The chief of police himself, in a moment of forgetfulness, was the first to betray himself. When Ivan Nikiforovich was informed of it, he said nothing: he merely inquired, "Was it the brown one?"

But Agafya Fedosyevna, who was present, began again to urge Ivan Nikiforovich. "What's the matter with you, Ivan Nikiforovich? People will laugh at you as at a fool if you let it pass. How can you remain a nobleman after that? You will be worse than the old woman who sells the honey-cakes with hemp-seed oil, you are so fond of." And the mischief-maker persuaded him. She hunted up somewhere a middle-aged man with black complexion, and spots all over his face, and a dark-blue surtout patched on the elbows—a regular official scribbler. He blacked his boots with tar, wore three pens behind his ear, and a glass bubble tied to his button-hole with a string, instead of an ink-bottle: he ate as many as nine pies at once, and put the tenth in his pocket, and wrote so many slanders of all sorts on a single sheet of stamped paper, that no reader could get through all at one time without interspersing coughs and sneezes. This poor imitation of a man labored, toiled, and wrote, and finally concocted the following document:

"To the District Judge of Mirgorod, from the noble, Ivan Dovgoch-khun, son of Nikifor.

"In pursuance of my petition which was presented by me, Ivan Dovgochkhun, son of Nikifor, in connection with the nobleman Ivan Pererépenko, son of Ivan; to which also, the judge of the Mirgorod district court exhibited his indifference. And the shameless, high-handed deed of the brown sow being kept secret, and coming to my ears from outside parties.

"And the said allowing and neglect, plainly malicious, lies incontestably at the judge's door; for the sow is a stupid animal, and therefore less fitted for the theft of papers. From which it plainly appears, that the said frequently mentioned sow was not otherwise than instigated to the same by the opponent, Ivan Pererépenko, son of Ivan, calling himself a nobleman, and already convicted of theft, conspiracy against life, and desecration of a church. But the said Mirgorod judge, with the partisanship peculiar to him, gave his private consent to this individual; for without such consent the said sow could by no possible means have been admitted to carry off the document; for the judge of the district court of Mirgorod is well provided with servants: it was only necessary to summon a soldier, who is always on duty in the reception-room, and who, although he has but one eye and one somewhat damaged arm, has powers quite adequate to driving out a sow, and to beating it with a club, from which is credibly evident the criminal neglect of the said Mirgorod judge, and the incontestable sharing of the Jew-like spoils therefrom resulting between these mutual conspirators. And the aforesaid robber and nobleman, Ivan Pererépenko, son of Ivan, having disgraced himself, finished his turning on his lathe. Wherefore I, the noble Ivan Dovgochkhun, son of Nikifor, declare to the said district judge, in proper form, that if the said brown sow, or the man Pererépenko, who was mentioned in the petition, in league with her, be not summoned to the court, and judgment in accordance with justice and my advantage pronounced upon her, then I, Ivan Dovgochkhun, son of Nikifor, shall present a complaint, with observance of all due formalities, against the said district judge, for his illegal partisanship, to the superior courts.

"Ivan Dovgochkhun, son of Nikifor, noble of the Mirgorod District."

This petition produced its effect. The judge was a man of timid disposition, as all good people generally are. He betook himself to the secretary. But the secretary emitted from his lips a thick *hm*, and exhibited in his countenance that indifferent and diabolically equivocal expression which Satan alone assumes when he sees his victim hasting to his feet. One resource remained—to reconcile the two friends. But how set about it, when all attempts up to that time had been so unsuccessful? Nevertheless, it was decided to make another effort; but Ivan Ivanovich declared downright that he would not hear to it, and even flew into a violent passion. Ivan Nikiforovich, in lieu of an answer, turned his back, and would not utter a word.

Then the case went on with the unusual promptness upon which courts usually pride themselves. Documents were dated, labelled, numbered, sewed together, registered, all in one day, and the matter laid on the shelf, where it continued to lie, lie, lie, for one, two, or three years. Many brides were married; a new street was laid out in Mirgorod; one of the judge's double teeth fell out, and two of his eye-teeth; more children than ever ran about Ivan Ivanovich's yard; Ivan Nikiforovich, as reproof to Ivan Ivanovich, had constructed a new goose-coop, although a little farther off than the first, and built himself completely off from Ivan Ivanovich, so that these worthy people almost never beheld each other's faces; and still the case lay on, in the very best order, in the cabinet, which had become marbled with ink-spots.

In the mean time a very important event for all Mirgorod had taken place. The chief of police had given a reception. Whence shall I obtain the brush and colors to depict this varied gathering, and this magnificent feast? Take your watch, open it, and observe what is going on there. A fearful confusion, is it not? Now, imagine almost the same, if not a greater, number of wheels standing in the chief of police's court-yard. How many brichkas [traps] and wagons were there! One was wide behind and narrow in front; another narrow behind and wide in front. One was a brichka and wagon combined; another neither a brichka nor a wagon. One resembled a huge hayrick, or a fat merchant's wife; another a dilapidated Jew, or a skeleton not quite freed from the skin. One was a perfect pipe with long stem in profile; another, resembling nothing whatever, suggested some strange, utterly formless, and exceedingly fantastic, being. In the midst of this chaos of wheels and carriage-boxes, rose the semblances of coaches, with windows like those of a room, crossed with broad frames.

The coachmen, in gray Cossack coats, svitkas [tunics], and white hare coats, with sheepskin hats and caps of various patterns, and pipes in their hands, drove the unharnessed horses through the yard. What a reception the chief of police gave! Permit me to run through the list of those who were there: Taras Tarasovich, Evpl Akinfovich, Evtikhii Evtikhievich, Ivan Ivanovich—not that Ivan Ivanovich, but another—Gabba Gavrilonovich, our Ivan Ivanovich, Elevferii Elevferievich, Makar Nazarevich, Foma Grigorovich . . . I can do no more: my powers fail me, my hand ceases to write.

And how many ladies were there! dark and fair and short, fat like Ivan Nikiforovich, and some so thin that it seemed as though each one might hide herself in the scabbard of the chief's sword. What head-dresses! what costumes!—red, yellow, coffee-color, green, blue, new, turned, made over—dresses, ribbons, reticules. Farewell, poor eyes! you will never be good for any thing any more after this spectacle.

And how long the table was drawn out! and how all talked! and what a humming they made! What is a mill with its driving-wheel, stones, beams, hammers, wheels, in comparison with this? I cannot tell you exactly what they talked about, but presumably of many agreeable and useful things, such as the weather, dogs, wheat, caps, and dice. At length Ivan Ivanovich—not that Ivan Ivanovich, but the other, who had but one eye—said, "It strikes me as strange that my right eye [one-eyed Ivan Ivanovich always spoke sarcastically about himself] does not see Ivan Nikiforovich, Mr. Dovgochkhun."

"He would not come," said the chief of police.

"Why not?"

"It's two years now, glory to God! since they quarrelled; that is, Ivan Ivanovich and Ivan Nikiforovich: and where one goes, the other will not go."

"You don't say so!" Thereupon one-eyed Ivan Ivanovich raised his eye, and clasped his hands. "Well, if people with good eyes cannot live in peace, how am I to live amicably, with my bad eye?" At these words, all laughed at the tops of their voices. All loved one-eyed Ivan Ivanovich, because he cracked jokes quite in the style of the present one. A tall, thin man in a frieze coat, with a plaster on his nose, who up to this time had sat in the corner, and never once altered the expression of his face, even when a fly lighted on his nose—this gentleman rose from his seat, and approached nearer to the crowd which surrounded one-eyed Ivan Ivanovich. "Listen," said one-eyed Ivan Ivanovich, when he perceived that quite a throng had collected about him; "see here: instead of gazing at my bad eye, suppose we make peace between our friends. Ivan Ivanovich is talking with the women and girls; . . . let us go quietly for Ivan Nikiforovich, and bring them together."

Ivan Ivanovich's proposal was unanimously agreed to; and it was decided to send at once to Ivan Nikiforovich's house, and beg him, at any rate, to come to the chief of police's for dinner. But the difficult question as to who was to be intrusted with this weighty commission rendered all thoughtful. They debated long as to who was the most fitted for, and expert in, diplomatic matters. At length it was unanimously agreed to depute Anton Prokofievich Golopuz for this business.

But it is necessary, first of all, to make the reader somewhat acquainted with this noteworthy person. Anton Prokofievich was a truly virtuous man, in the fullest meaning of the term. If any one in Mirgorod gives him a neckerchief or underclothes, he returns thanks; if any one gives him a fillip on the nose—he returns thanks then also. If he was asked, "Why, Anton Prokofievich, have you a light brown coat with blue sleeves?" he generally replied, "Ah, you haven't one like it! Wait: it will wear off, and it will be alike all over." And, in point of fact, the blue cloth, from the effects of the sun, began to turn cinnamon-color, and had now become of the same tint as the rest of the coat. But the strange part of it was that Anton Prokofievich had a habit of wearing woollen clothing in summer and nankeen in winter. Anton Prokofievich has no house of his own. He used to have one at the extremity of the town; but he sold it, and with the purchase-money bought a troika [three-horse carriage] of brown horses, and a little brichka in which he drove about to stay with the squires. But as the horses made a good deal of trouble, and money was required for oats, Anton Prokofievich swapped them off for a violin and a house-maid, with twenty-five paper rubles to boot. Afterwards Anton Prokofievich sold the violin, and swapped the girl for a morocco and gold tobacco-pouch; and now he has such a tobacco-pouch as no one else has. As a result of this luxury, he can no longer go about among the country-houses, but must remain in the city, and pass the night at different houses, especially of those gentlemen who take pleasure in tapping him on the nose. Anton Prokofievich is very fond of good eating, and plays well at *durak* and *melnik*.* Obeying orders always was his forte; so, taking his hat and cane, he set out at once on his way.

But, as he walked along, he began to ponder in what manner he should contrive to induce Ivan Nikiforovich to come to the assembly. The rather unbending character of the latter, who was otherwise a worthy man, rendered his undertaking almost hopeless. Yes, and how, in fact, was he to persuade him to come, when even rising from his bed cost him so great an effort? But supposing that he does rise, how can he get him there, where, as he doubtless knows, his irreconcilable enemy already is? The more Anton Prokofievich reflected, the more difficulties he perceived. The day was sultry, the sun beat down, the perspiration poured from him in streams. Anton Prokofievich was a tolerably sharp man in many respects (though they did tap him on the nose). In swapping, however, he was not fortunate. He knew very well when to play the fool, and sometimes contrived to turn things to his own profit, amid circumstances and surroundings from which a wise man could rarely escape without loss.

His ingenious mind had contrived a means of persuading Ivan Niki-forovich; and he was proceeding bravely to face everything, when an unexpected occurrence somewhat disturbed his equanimity. There is no harm, at this point, in admitting to the reader, that, among other things, Anton Prokofievich was the owner of a pair of trousers of such singular properties, that, when he put them on, the dogs always bit his calves. Unfortunately, on this day he had donned that particular pair of trousers; and so he had hardly resigned himself to meditation when a fearful barking on all sides saluted his ears. Anton Prokofievich raised such a yell

---

* Card games: literally, "fool" and "miller."—TRANSLATOR.

(no one could scream louder than he) that not only did the well-known woman and the inhabitant of the endless surtout rush out to meet him, but even the small boys from Ivan Ivanovich's yard strewed themselves over him; and although the dogs succeeded in tasting only one of his calves, yet this sensibly diminished his courage, and he entered the veranda with a certain amount of timidity.

VII. and Last.

"AH! HOW do you do? Why do you irritate the dogs?" said Ivan Nikiforovich, on perceiving Anton Prokofievich; for no one spoke otherwise than jestingly with Anton Prokofievich.

"Hang them! who's been irritating them?" retorted Anton Prokofievich.

"You lie!"

"By Heavens, no!—You are invited to dinner by Peter Feodorovich."

"Hm!"

"He invited you more pressingly than I can tell you. 'Why,' says he, 'does Ivan Nikiforovich shun me like an enemy? He never comes round to have a chat, or make a call.' "

Ivan Nikiforovich stroked his beard.

" 'If,' says he, 'Ivan Nikiforovich does not come now, I shall not know what to think: surely, he must have some design against me. Pray, Anton Prokofievich, persuade Ivan Nikiforovich!' Come, Ivan Nikiforovich, let us go! a very choice company is already assembled there."

Ivan Nikiforovich began to regard a cock, which was perched on the roof, and crowing with all its might.

"If you only knew, Ivan Nikiforovich," pursued the zealous ambassador, "what fresh sturgeon and caviare Peter Feodorovich has had sent to him!" Whereupon Ivan Nikiforovich turned his head, and began to listen attentively. This encouraged the messenger. "Come quick: Foma Grigorovich is there too. Why don't you come?" he added, seeing that Ivan Nikiforovich still lay in the same position. "Why, shall we go, or not?"

"I won't!"

This "I won't" startled Anton Prokofievich: he had fancied that his alluring representations had quite moved this very worthy man; but instead, he heard that decisive "I won't."

"Why won't you?" he asked, almost with vexation, which he very rarely exhibited, even when they put burning paper on his head, a trick which the judge and the chief of police were particularly fond of indulging in.

Ivan Nikiforovich took a pinch of snuff.

"As you like, Ivan Nikiforovich. I do not know what detains you."

"Why won't I go?" said Ivan Nikiforovich at length: "that brigand will be there!" This was his ordinary way of alluding to Ivan Ivanovich. "Just God! and is it long" . . .

"He will not be there, he will not be there! May the lightning kill me on the spot!" returned Anton Prokofievich, who was ready to perjure himself ten times in an hour. "Come along, Ivan Nikiforovich!"

"Yes, you lie, Anton Prokofievich! he is there!"

"By Heavens, by Heavens, he's not! May I never stir from this place if he's there! Now, just think for yourself, what object have I in lying? May my hands and feet wither! . . . Why, don't you believe me now? May I perish right here in your presence! Don't you believe me yet?"

Ivan Nikiforovich was entirely re-assured by these asseverations, and ordered his valet, in the boundless surtout, to fetch his trousers and nankeen casaquin.

I suppose that to describe how Ivan Nikiforovich put on his trousers, how they wound his neckerchief about his neck, and finally dragged on his casaquin, which burst under the left sleeve, would be quite superfluous. Suffice it to say that during all that time he preserved a becoming calmness of demeanor, and answered not a word to Anton Prokofievich's proposition to swap something for his Turkish tobacco-pouch.

Meanwhile the assembly awaited with impatience the decisive moment when Ivan Nikiforovich should make his appearance, and at length comply with the general desire, that these worthy people should be reconciled to each other. Many were almost convinced that Ivan Nikiforovich would not come. Even the chief of police offered to bet with one-eyed Ivan Ivanovich that he would not come; and he only desisted because one-eyed Ivan Ivanovich demanded that he should wager his shot foot against his own bad eye, at which the chief of police was greatly offended, and the company enjoyed a quiet laugh. No one had yet sat down to the table, although it was long past two o'clock, an hour before which in Mirgorod, even on ceremonious occasions, every one had already long dined.

No sooner did Anton Prokofievich show himself in the doorway than he was instantly surrounded by all. Anton Prokofievich, in answer to all inquiries, shouted one all-decisive word, "He will not come!" No sooner had he uttered this, than a hailstorm of reproaches, scoldings, and, possibly, even fillips, prepared to descend upon his head for the ill success of his mission, when all at once the door opened, and—Ivan Nikiforovich entered.

If Satan himself or a corpse had appeared, it would not have caused such consternation throughout the company as Ivan Nikiforovich's unexpected arrival created. But Anton Prokofievich only went off into a fit of laughter, and held his sides with delight at having played such a joke upon the company.

At all events, it was almost past the belief of all that Ivan Nikiforovich could, in so brief a space of time, have attired himself like a respectable gentleman. Ivan Ivanovich was not there at the moment: he had stepped out somewhere. Recovering from their amazement, the public took an interest in Ivan Nikiforovich's health, and expressed their pleasure at his increase in breadth. Ivan Nikiforovich kissed every one, and said, "Very much obliged!"

Meantime the fragrance of the beet-soup was wafted through the apartment, and tickled the nostrils of the hungry guests very agreeably. All rushed headlong to the table. The line of ladies, loquacious and silent, thin and thick, swept on, and the long table glittered with all the hues of the rainbow. I will not describe the courses: I will make no mention of the curd dumplings with sour cream, nor of the dish of haslets that was served with the soup, nor of the turkey with plums and raisins, nor of the dish which greatly resembled in appearance a boot soaked in kvas, nor of the sauce, which is the swan's song of the old-fashioned cook, nor of that other sauce which was brought in all enveloped in the flames of wine, which amused as well as frightened the ladies extremely. I will say nothing of these dishes, because I like better to eat them than to spend many words in discussing them.

Ivan Ivanovich was exceedingly pleased with the fish prepared with horseradish. He devoted himself particularly to this useful and nourishing preparation. Picking out all the fine bones from the fish, he laid them on his plate; and happening to glance across the table . . . Heavenly Creator! but this was strange! Opposite him sat Ivan Nikiforovich.

At the very same instant Ivan Nikiforovich glanced up also . . . No . . . I can do no more . . . Give me a fresh pen! My pen is flabby, dead, . . . with a fine point for this picture! Their faces seemed to turn to stone, still keeping their defiant expression. Each beheld a long familiar face, to which it seemed the most natural of things to step up as to an unexpected friend, involuntarily, and offer a snuff-box, with the words, "Do me the favor," or "Dare I beg you to do me the favor?" Instead of this, that face was terrible as a forerunner of evil. The perspiration poured in streams from Ivan Ivanovich and Ivan Nikiforovich.

All the guests at table grew dumb with attention, and never took their eyes from the former friends. The ladies, who had been busy up to that time with a sufficiently interesting discussion as to the preparation of capons, suddenly cut their conversation short. All was silence. It was a picture worthy the brush of a great artist.

At length Ivan Ivanovich pulled out his handkerchief, and began to blow his nose; but Ivan Nikiforovich glanced about, and his eye rested on the open door. The chief of police at once perceived this movement, and ordered the door to be strongly fastened. Then both of the friends began to eat, and never once glanced at each other again.

As soon as dinner was done, both of the former friends rose from their seats, and began to look for their hats, with a view to departure. Then the chief beckoned; and Ivan Ivanovich—not that Ivan Ivanovich, but the other, the one with the one eye—stood behind Ivan Nikiforovich, and the chief stepped behind Ivan Ivanovich, and both began to drag them backwards, in order to bring them together, and not release them until they had shaken hands with each other. Ivan Ivanovich, the one-eyed Ivan, pushed Ivan Nikiforovich, though rather crookedly, yet with tolerable success, towards the spot where stood Ivan Ivanovich; but the chief of police directed his course too much to one side, because he could not steer himself with his refractory leg, which obeyed no orders whatever on this occasion, and, as if with malice aforethought, swung itself uncommonly far, and in quite the contrary direction (which possibly resulted from the fact that there had been an unusual amount of fruit-wine after dinner), so that Ivan Ivanovich fell over a lady in a red gown, who had thrust herself into the very centre, out of curiosity. Such an omen foreboded nothing good. Nevertheless, the judge, in order to set the matter to rights, took the chief of police's place, and, sweeping all the snuff from his upper lip with his nose, pushed Ivan Ivanovich in the opposite direction. In Mirgorod this is the usual manner of effecting a reconciliation: it somewhat resembles a game of ball. As soon as the judge pushed Ivan Ivanovich, Ivan Ivanovich with the one eye exerted all his strength, and pushed Ivan Nikiforovich, from whom the perspiration streamed like rain-water from the roofs. In spite of the fact that the friends resisted to the best of their ability, nevertheless they were brought together, for the two active movers received re-enforcements from the ranks of the guests.

Then they were closely surrounded on all sides, not to be released until they had decided to give each other their hands. "God be with you, Ivan Nikiforovich and Ivan Ivanovich! declare upon your honor now, what you quarrelled about; trifles, wasn't it? aren't you ashamed of yourselves before people and before God?"

"I do not know," said Ivan Nikiforovich, panting with fatigue (it is to be observed that he was not at all disinclined to a reconciliation), "I do not know what I did to Ivan Ivanovich; but why did he destroy my coop, and plot against my life?"

"I am innocent of any evil designs!" said Ivan Ivanovich, never looking at Ivan Nikiforovich. "I swear before God and before you, honorable noblemen, I did nothing to my enemy! Why does he calumniate me, and injure my rank and family?"

"What injury have I done you, Ivan Ivanovich?" said Ivan Nikiforovich. One moment more of explanation, and the long enmity was on the point of being extinguished. Ivan Nikiforovich was already feeling in his pocket for his snuff-box, and was about to say, "Do me the favor."

"Is it no injury," answered Ivan Ivanovich, without raising his eyes, "when you, my dear sir, insulted my honor and my family with a word which it is improper to repeat here?"

"Permit me to observe, in a friendly manner, Ivan Ivanovich (here Ivan Nikiforovich touched Ivan Ivanovich's button with his finger, which clearly indicated the disposition of his mind), that you took offence, the deuce only knows at what, because I called you a *goose*." . . .

It came over Ivan Nikiforovich that he had made a mistake in uttering that word; but it was too late: the word was out. Everything went to the deuce. If, on the utterance of this word without witnesses, Ivan Ivanovich lost control of himself, and flew into such a passion as God preserve us from beholding any man in, what was to be expected now? I put it to you, dear readers, what was to be expected now, when the fatal word was uttered in an assemblage of persons among whom were ladies, in whose presence Ivan Ivanovich liked to be particularly polite? If Ivan Nikiforovich had set to work in any other manner, if he had only said *bird* and not *goose*, it might still have been arranged; but . . . all was at an end.

He cast one glance upon Ivan Nikiforovich, and such a glance! If that glance had possessed active power, then it would have turned Ivan Nikiforovich into dust. The guests understood the glance, and hastened to separate them. And this man, the very model of gentleness, who never let a single poor woman go without interrogating her, rushed out in a fearful rage. Such violent storms do passions produce!

For a whole month nothing was heard of Ivan Ivanovich. He shut himself up at home. His ancestral chest was opened; from the chest was taken—what? silver rubles, his grandfather's old silver rubles! And these rubles passed into the ink-stained hands of legal advisers. The case was sent up to the higher court; and when Ivan Ivanovich received the joyful news that it would be decided on the morrow, then only did he look out upon the world, and resolve to emerge from his house. Alas! from that time forth, the council gave notice day by day, that the case would be finished on the morrow, for the space of ten years.

Five years ago, I passed through the town of Mirgorod. I came at a bad time. It was autumn, with its damp, melancholy weather, mud and mists. An unnatural verdure, the result of tiresome and incessant rains, covered with a watery network the fields and meadows, to which it is as well suited as youthful pranks to an old man, or roses to an old woman. The weather made a deep impression on me at that time: when it was dull, I was dull; but in spite of that, when I came to pass through Mirgorod, my heart beat violently. God, what reminiscences! I had not beheld Mirgorod for twenty years. Here then had lived, in touching friendship, two inseparable friends. And how many prominent people had died! Judge Demyan Demyanovich was already gone: Ivan Ivanovich (with the one eye) had long ceased to live. I entered the main street. All about stood poles with bundles of straw on top: some new grading was being done. Several izbás had been removed. The remnants of board and wattled fences projected sadly, here and there.

It was a festival day. I ordered my basket kibitka [hooded cart] to stop in front of the church, and entered softly that no one might turn round. To tell the truth, there was no need of this: the church was empty; there were very few people; it was evident that even the most pious feared the mud. The candles seemed strangely unpleasant in that gloomy, or, better still, sickly, light. The dim vestibule was melancholy; the long windows, with their circular panes, were bedewed with tears of rain; I retired into the vestibule, and addressed myself to a respectable old man, with grayish hair: "May I inquire if Ivan Nikiforovich is still living?" At that moment the lamp before the ikon burned up more brightly, and the light fell directly upon the face of my companion. What was my surprise, on looking more closely, to behold features with which I was acquainted! It was Ivan Nikiforovich himself! But how he had changed!

"Are you well, Ivan Nikiforovich? How old you have grown!"

"Yes, I have grown old. I have just come from Poltava to-day," answered Ivan Nikiforovich.

"You don't say so! you have been to Poltava in this bad weather?"

"What was to be done? that lawsuit" . . .

At this I sighed involuntarily.

Ivan Nikiforovich observed my sigh, and said, "Do not be troubled: I have reliable information that the case will be decided next week, and in my favor."

I shrugged my shoulders, and went to get some news of Ivan Ivanovich.

"Ivan Ivanovich is here," some one said to me, "in the choir."

Then I saw a gaunt form. Was that Ivan Ivanovich? His face was covered with wrinkles, his hair was perfectly white; but the bekesha was the same as ever. After the first greetings were over, Ivan Ivanovich, turning to me with the joyous smile which always became his funnel-shaped face, said, "Have you been informed of the pleasant news?"

"What news?" I inquired.

"My case is to be decided to-morrow without fail: the court has announced it decisively."

I sighed more deeply than before, and made haste to take my leave (for I was bound on very important business), and seated myself in my kibitka.

The lean nags known in Mirgorod as "courier's horses" started, producing with their hoofs, which were buried in a gray mass of mud, a sound very displeasing to the ear. The rain poured in torrents upon the Jew seated on the box, covered with a rug. The dampness penetrated through and through me. The gloomy barrier with a sentry-box, in which an old soldier was repairing his gray weapons, passed slowly by. Again the same fields, in some places black where they had been dug up, in others of a greenish hue; wet daws and crows; monotonous rain; a tearful sky, without one gleam of light! . . . It is dull in this world, gentlemen!

The Nose

I

On March 25th there took place, in Petersburg, an extraordinarily strange occurrence. The barber Ivan Yakovlevich, who lives on Voznesensky Avenue (his family name has been lost and even on his signboard, where a gentleman is depicted with a lathered cheek and the inscription "Also bloodletting," there is nothing else)—the barber Ivan Yakovlevich woke up rather early and smelled fresh bread. Raising himself slightly in bed he saw his spouse, a rather respectable lady who was very fond of drinking coffee, take some newly baked loaves out of the oven.

"I won't have any coffee to-day, Praskovya Osipovna," said Ivan Yakovlevich. "Instead, I would like to eat a bit of hot bread with onion." (That is to say, Ivan Yakovlevich would have liked both the one and the other, but he knew that it was quite impossible to demand two things at once, for Praskovya Osipovna very much disliked such whims.) "Let the fool eat the bread; all the better for me," the wife thought to herself, "there will be an extra cup of coffee left." And she threw a loaf onto the table.

For the sake of propriety Ivan Yakovlevich put a tailcoat on over his shirt and, sitting down at the table, poured out some salt, got two onions ready, picked up a knife and, assuming a meaningful expression, began to slice the bread. Having cut the loaf in two halves, he looked inside and to his astonishment saw something white. Ivan Yakovlevich poked it carefully with the knife and felt it with his finger. "Solid!" he said to himself. "What could it be?"

He stuck in his finger and extracted—a nose! Ivan Yakovlevich was dumbfounded. He rubbed his eyes and felt the object: a nose, a nose indeed, and a familiar one at that. Ivan Yakovlevich's face expressed horror. But this horror was nothing compared to the indignation which seized his spouse.

"You beast, where did you cut off a nose?" she shouted angrily. "Scoundrel! drunkard! I'll report you to the police myself. What a ruffian! I have already heard from three people that you jerk their noses about so much when shaving that it's a wonder they stay in place."

But Ivan Yakovlevich was more dead than alive. He recognized the nose as that of none other than Collegiate Assessor Kovalyov, whom he shaved every Wednesday and Sunday.

"Hold on, Praskovya Osipovna! I shall put it in a corner, after I've wrapped it in a rag: let it lie there for a while, and later I'll take it away."

"I won't even hear of it. That I should allow a cut-off nose to lie about in my room? You dry stick! All he knows is how to strop his razor, but soon he'll be in no condition to carry out his duty, the rake, the villain! Am I to answer for you to the police? You piece of filth, you blockhead! Away with it! Away! Take it anywhere you like! Out of my sight with it!"

Ivan Yakovlevich stood there as though bereft of senses. He thought and thought—and really did not know what to think. "The devil knows how it happened," he said at last, scratching behind his ear with his hand. "Was I drunk or wasn't I when I came home yesterday, I really can't say. Whichever way you look at it, this is an impossible occurrence. After all, bread is something baked, and a nose is something altogether different. I can't make it out at all."

Ivan Yakovlevich fell silent. The idea that the police might find the nose in his possession and bring a charge against him drove him into a complete frenzy. He was already visualizing the scarlet collar, beautifully embroidered with silver, the saber—and he trembled all over. At last he got out his underwear and boots, pulled on all these tatters and, followed by rather weighty exhortations from Praskovya Osipovna, wrapped the nose in a rag and went out into the street.

He wanted to shove it under something somewhere, either into the hitching-post by the gate—or just drop it as if by accident and then turn off into a side street. But as bad luck would have it, he kept running into people he knew, who at once would ask him, "Where are you going?" or "Whom are you going to shave so early?", so that Ivan Yakovlevich couldn't find the right moment. Once he actually did drop it, but a policeman some distance away pointed to it with his halberd and said: "Pick it up—you've dropped something there," and Ivan Yakovlevich was obliged to pick up the nose and hide it in his pocket. He was seized with despair, all the more so as the number of people in the street constantly increased when the shops began to open.

He decided to go to St. Isaac's Bridge—might he not just manage to toss it into the Neva? But I am somewhat to blame for having so far said nothing about Ivan Yakovlevich, in many ways a respectable man.

Like any self-respecting Russian artisan, Ivan Yakovlevich was a terrible drunkard. And although every day he shaved other people's chins his own was ever unshaven. Ivan Yakovlevich's tailcoat (Ivan Yakovlevich never wore a frockcoat) was piebald, that is to say, it was all black but dappled with brownish-yellow and gray; the collar was shiny, and in place of three of the buttons hung just the ends of thread. Ivan Yakovlevich was a great cynic, and when Collegiate Assessor Kovalyov told him while being shaved, "Your hands, Ivan Yakovlevich, always stink," Ivan Yakovlevich would reply with the question, "Why should they stink?" "I don't know, my dear fellow," the Collegiate Assessor would say, "but they do," and Ivan Yakovlevich, after taking a pinch of snuff, would, in retaliation, lather all over his cheeks and under his nose, and behind his ear, and under his chin—in other words, wherever his fancy took him.

This worthy citizen now found himself on St. Isaac's Bridge. To begin with, he took a good look around, then leaned on the railings as though to look under the bridge to see whether or not there were many fish swimming about, and surreptitiously tossed down the rag containing the nose. He felt as though all of a sudden a ton had been lifted off him: Ivan Yakovlevich even smirked. Instead of going to shave some civil servants' chins he set off for an establishment bearing a sign "Snacks and Tea" to order a glass of punch when he suddenly noticed, at the end of the bridge, a police officer of distinguished appearance, with wide sideburns, wearing a three-cornered hat and with a sword. His heart sank: the officer was wagging his finger at him and saying, "Step this way, my friend."

Knowing the etiquette, Ivan Yakovlevich removed his cap while still some way off, and approaching with alacrity said, "I wish your honor good health."

"No, no, my good fellow, not 'your honor.' Just you tell me, what were you doing over there, standing on the bridge?"

"Honestly, sir, I've been to shave someone and only looked to see if the river were running fast."

"You're lying, you're lying. This won't do. Just be so good as to answer."

"I am ready to shave your worship twice a week, or even three times, and no complaints," replied Ivan Yakovlevich.

"No, my friend, all that's nonsense. I have three barbers who shave me and deem it a great honor, too. Just be so good as to tell me, what were you doing over there?"

Ivan Yakovlevich turned pale. . . . But here the whole episode becomes shrouded in mist, and of what happened subsequently absolutely nothing is known.

II

COLLEGIATE ASSESSOR Kovalyov woke up rather early and made a "b-rr-rr" sound with his lips as he was wont to do on awakening, although he could not have explained the reason for it. Kovalyov stretched and asked for the small mirror standing on the table. He wanted to have a look at the pimple which had, the evening before, appeared on his nose. But to his extreme amazement he saw that he had, in the place of his nose, a perfectly smooth surface. Frightened, Kovalyov called for some water and rubbed his eyes with a towel: indeed, no nose! He ran his hand over himself to see whether or not he was asleep. No, he didn't think so. The Collegiate Assessor jumped out of bed and shook himself—no nose! He at once ordered his clothes to be brought to him, and flew off straight to the chief of police.

In the meantime something must be said about Kovalyov, to let the reader see what sort of man this collegiate assessor was. Collegiate assessors who receive their rank on the strength of scholarly diplomas can by no means be equated with those who make the rank in the Caucasus. They are two entirely different breeds. Learned collegiate assessors . . . But Russia is such a wondrous land that if you say something about one collegiate assessor all the collegiate assessors from Riga to Kamchatka will not fail to take it as applying to them, too. The same is true of all our ranks and titles. Kovalyov belonged to the Caucasus variety of collegiate assessors. He had only held that rank for two years and therefore could not forget it for a moment; and in order to lend himself added dignity and weight he never referred to himself as collegiate assessor but always as major. "Listen, my dear woman," he would usually say on meeting in the street a woman selling shirt fronts, "come to my place, my apartment is on Sadovaya; just ask where Major Kovalyov lives, anyone will show you." And if the woman he met happened to be a pretty one, he would also give some confidential instructions, adding, "You just ask, lovey, for Major Kovalyov's apartment."—That is why we, too, will henceforth refer to this collegiate assessor as Major.

Major Kovalyov was in the habit of taking a daily stroll along Nevsky Avenue. The collar of his dress shirt was always exceedingly clean and starched. His sidewhiskers were of the kind you can still see on provincial and district surveyors, or architects (provided they are Russians), as well as on those individuals who perform various police duties, and in general on all those men who have full rosy cheeks and are very good at boston; these sidewhiskers run along the middle of the cheek straight up to the nose. Major Kovalyov wore a great many cornelian seals, some with crests and others with Wednesday, Thursday, Monday, etc., engraved on them. Major Kovalyov had come to Petersburg on business, to wit, to look for a post befitting his rank; if he could arrange it, that of a vice-governor; otherwise, that of a procurement officer in some important government department. Major Kovalyov was not averse to getting married, but only in the event that the bride had a fortune of two hundred thousand. And therefore the reader can now judge for himself what this major's state was when he saw, in the place of a fairly presentable and moderate-sized nose, a most ridiculous flat and smooth surface.

As bad luck would have it, not a single cab showed up in the street, and he was forced to walk, wrapped up in his cloak, his face covered with a handkerchief, pretending that his nose was bleeding. "But perhaps I just imagined all this—a nose cannot disappear in this idiotic way." He stepped into a coffee-house just in order to look at himself in a mirror. Fortunately, there was no one there. Serving boys were sweeping the rooms and arranging the chairs; some of them, sleepy-eyed, were bringing out trays of hot turnovers; yesterday's papers, coffee-stained, lay about on tables and chairs. "Well, thank God, there is no one here," said the Major. "Now I can have a look." Timidly he approached the mirror and glanced at it. "Damnation! How disgusting!" he exclaimed after spitting. "If at least there were something in place of the nose, but there's nothing!"

Biting his lips with annoyance, he left the coffee-house and decided, contrary to his habit, not to look or to smile at anyone. Suddenly he stopped dead in his tracks before the door of a house. An inexplicable phenomenon took place before his very eyes: a carriage drew up to the entrance; the doors opened; a gentleman in uniform jumped out, slightly stooping, and ran up the stairs. Imagine the horror and at the same time the amazement of Kovalyov when he recognized that it was his own nose! At this extraordinary sight everything seemed to whirl before his eyes; he felt that he could hardly keep on his feet. Trembling all over as though with fever, he made up his mind, come what may, to await the gentleman's return to the carriage. Two minutes later the Nose indeed came out. He was wearing a gold-embroidered uniform with a big stand-up collar and doeskin breeches; there was a sword at his side. From his plumed hat one could infer that he held the rank of a state councillor. Everything pointed to his being on the way to pay a call. He looked right and left, shouted to his driver, "Bring the carriage round," got in and was driven off.

Poor Kovalyov almost went out of his mind. He did not even know what to think of this strange occurrence. Indeed, how could a nose which as recently as yesterday had been on his face and could neither ride nor walk—how could it be in uniform? He ran after the carriage, which fortunately had not gone far but had stopped before the Kazan Cathedral.

He hurried into the cathedral, made his way past the ranks of old beggarwomen with bandaged faces and two slits for their eyes, whom he used to make such fun of, and went inside. There were but few worshippers there: they all stood by the entrance. Kovalyov felt so upset that he was in no condition to pray and searched with his eyes for the gentleman in all the church corners. At last he saw him standing to one side. The Nose had completely hidden his face in his big stand-up collar and was praying in an attitude of utmost piety.

"How am I to approach him?" thought Kovalyov. "From everything, from his uniform, from his hat, one can see that he is a state councillor. I'll be damned if I know how to do it."

He started clearing his throat, but the Nose never changed his devout attitude and continued his genuflections.

"My dear sir," said Kovalyov, forcing himself to take courage, "my dear sir . . ."

"What is it you desire?" said the Nose turning round.

"It is strange, my dear sir . . . I think . . . you ought to know your place. And all of a sudden I find you—and where? In church. You'll admit . . ."

"Excuse me, I cannot understand what you are talking about. . . . Make yourself clear."

"How shall I explain to him?" thought Kovalyov and, emboldened, began: "Of course, I . . . however, I am a major. For me to go about without my nose, you'll admit, is unbecoming. It's all right for a peddler woman who sells peeled oranges on Voskresensky Bridge, to sit without a nose. But since I'm expecting—and besides, having many acquaintances among the ladies—Mrs. Chekhtaryova, a state councillor's wife, and others . . . Judge for yourself . . . I don't know, my dear sir . . ." (Here Major Kovalyov shrugged his shoulders.) "Forgive me, if one were to look at this in accordance with rules of duty and honor . . . you yourself can understand. . . ."

"I understand absolutely nothing," replied the Nose. "Make yourself more clear."

"My dear sir," said Kovalyov with a sense of his own dignity, "I don't know how to interpret your words . . . The whole thing seems to me quite obvious . . . Or do you wish . . . After all, you are my own nose!"—

The Nose looked at the major and slightly knitted his brows.

"You are mistaken, my dear sir, I exist in my own right. Besides, there can be no close relation between us. Judging by the buttons on your uniform, you must be employed in the Senate or at least in the Ministry of Justice. As for me, I am in the scholarly line."

Having said this, the Nose turned away and went back to his prayers.

Kovalyov was utterly flabbergasted. He knew not what to do or even what to think. Just then he heard the pleasant rustle of a lady's dress: an elderly lady, all in lace, had come up near him and with her, a slim one, in a white frock which agreeably outlined her slender figure, and in a straw-colored hat, light as a cream-puff. Behind them, a tall footman with huge sidewhiskers and a whole dozen collars, stopped and opened a snuff-box.

Kovalyov stepped closer, pulled out the cambric collar of his dress shirt, adjusted his seals hanging on a golden chain and, smiling in all directions, turned his attention to the ethereal young lady who, like a spring flower, bowed her head slightly and put her little white hand with its translucent fingers to her forehead. The smile on Kovalyov's face grew even wider when from under her hat he caught a glimpse of her little round dazzling-white chin and part of her cheek glowing with the color of the first rose of spring. But suddenly he sprang back as though scalded. He remembered that there was absolutely nothing in the place of his nose, and tears came to his eyes. He turned round, intending without further ado to tell the gentleman in uniform that he was merely pretending to be a state councillor, that he was a rogue and a cad and nothing more than his, the major's, own nose. . . . But the Nose was no longer there; he had managed to dash off, probably to pay another call.

This plunged Kovalyov into despair. He went back, stopped for a moment under the colonnade and looked carefully, this way and that, for the Nose to turn up somewhere. He remembered quite well that the latter had a plumed hat and a gold-embroidered uniform, but he had not noticed his overcoat, or the color of his carriage or of his horses, not even whether he had a footman at the back, and if so in what livery. Moreover, there was such a multitude of carriages dashing back and forth and at such speed that it was difficult to tell them apart; but even if he did pick one of them out, he would have no means of stopping it. The day was fine and sunny. There were crowds of people on Nevsky Avenue. A whole flowery cascade of ladies poured over the sidewalk, all the way down from Police Bridge to Anichkin Bridge. Here came a court councillor he knew, and was used to addressing as lieutenant-colonel, especially in the presence of strangers. Here, too, was Yarygin, a head clerk in the Senate, a great friend of his, who invariably lost at boston when he went up eight. Here was another major who had won his assessorship in the Caucasus, waving to Kovalyov to join him. . . .

"O hell!" said Kovalyov. "Hey, cabby, take me straight to the chief of police!"

Kovalyov got into the cab and kept shouting to the cabman, "Get going as fast as you can."

"Is the chief of police at home?" he called out as he entered the hall.

"No, sir," answered the doorman, "he has just left."

"You don't say."

"Yes," added the doorman, "he has not been gone long, but he's gone. Had you come a minute sooner perhaps you might have found him in."

Without removing the handkerchief from his face, Kovalyov got back into the cab and in a voice of despair shouted, "Drive on!"

"Where to?" asked the cabman.

"Drive straight ahead!"

"What do you mean straight ahead? There is a turn here. Right or left?"

This question nonplussed Kovalyov and made him think again. In his plight the first thing for him to do was to apply to the Police Department, not because his case had anything to do directly with the police, but because they could act much more quickly than any other institution; while to seek satisfaction from the superiors of the department by which the Nose claimed to be employed would be pointless because from the Nose's own replies it was obvious that this fellow held nothing sacred, and that he was capable of lying in this case, too, as he had done when he had assured Kovalyov that they had never met. Thus Kovalyov was on the point of telling the cabman to take him to the Police Department when the thought again occurred to him that this rogue and swindler, who had already treated him so shamelessly during their first encounter, might again seize his first chance to slip out of town somewhere, and then all search would be futile or might drag on, God forbid, a whole month. Finally, it seemed, heaven itself brought him to his senses. He decided to go straight to the newspaper office and, before it was too late, place an advertisement with a detailed description of the Nose's particulars, so that anyone coming across him could immediately deliver him or at least give information about his whereabouts. And so, his mind made up, he told the cabby to drive to the newspaper office, and all the way down to it kept whacking him in the back with his fist, saying, "Faster, you villain! faster, you rogue!"—"Ugh, mister!" the cabman would say, shaking his head and flicking his reins at the horse whose coat was as long as a lapdog's. At last the cab drew up to a stop, and Kovalyov, panting, ran into a small reception room where a gray-haired clerk in an old tailcoat and glasses sat at a table and, pen in his teeth, counted newly brought in coppers.

"Who accepts advertisements here?" cried Kovalyov. "Ah, good morning!"

"How do you do," said the gray-haired clerk, raising his eyes for a moment and lowering them again to look at the neat stacks of money.

"I should like to insert—"

"Excuse me. Will you wait a moment," said the clerk as he wrote down a figure on a piece of paper with one hand and moved two beads on the abacus with the fingers of his left hand. A liveried footman, whose appearance suggested his sojourn in an aristocratic house, and who stood by the table with a note in his hand, deemed it appropriate to demonstrate his savoir-faire: "Would you believe it, sir, this little mutt is not worth eighty kopecks, that is, I wouldn't even give eight kopecks for it; but the countess loves it, honestly she does—and so whoever finds it will get one hundred rubles! To put it politely, just as you and I are talking, people's tastes differ: if you're a hunter, keep a pointer or a poodle; don't grudge five hundred, give a thousand, but then let it be a good dog."

The worthy clerk listened to this with a grave expression while at the same time trying to count the number of letters in the note brought to him. All around stood a great many old women, salespeople and house porters with notes. One of them offered for sale a coachman of sober conduct; another, a little-used carriage brought from Paris in 1814; still others, a nineteen-year-old serf girl experienced in laundering work and suitable for other kinds of work; a sound droshky with one spring missing; a young and fiery dappled-gray horse seventeen years old; turnip and radish seed newly received from London; a summer residence with all the appurtenances—to wit, two stalls for horses and a place for planting a grove of birches or firs; there was also an appeal to those wishing to buy old boot soles, inviting them to appear for final bidding every day between eight and three o'clock. The room in which this entire company was crowded was small, and the air in it was extremely thick; but Collegiate Assessor Kovalyov was not in a position to notice the smell, because he kept his handkerchief pressed to his face and because his nose itself was goodness knows where.

"My dear sir, may I ask you . . . It is very urgent," he said at last with impatience.

"Presently, presently! Two rubles forty-three kopecks! Just a moment! One ruble sixty-four kopecks," recited the gray-haired gentleman, tossing the notes into the faces of the old women and the house porters. "What can I do for you?" he said at last, turning to Kovalyov.

"I wish . . . ," said Kovalyov. "There has been a swindle or a fraud . . . I still can't find out. I just wish to advertise that whoever hands this scoundrel over to me will receive an adequate reward."

"Allow me to inquire, what is your name?"

"What do you want my name for? I can't give it to you. I have many acquaintances: Mrs. Chekhtaryova, the wife of a state councillor; Pelageya Grigoryevna Podtochina, the wife of a field officer . . . What if they suddenly were to find out? Heaven forbid! You can simply write down: a collegiate assessor or, still better, a person holding the rank of major."

"And was the runaway your household serf?"

"What do you mean, household serf? That wouldn't be such a bad swindle! The runaway was . . . my nose. . . ."

"Hmm! what a strange name! And did this Mr. Nosov rob you of a big sum?"

"My nose, I mean to say—You've misunderstood me. My nose, my very own nose has disappeared goodness knows where. The devil must have wished to play a trick on me!"

"But how did it disappear? I don't quite understand it."

"Well, I can't tell you how; but the main thing is that it is now gallivanting about town and calling itself a state councillor. And that is why I am asking you to advertise that whoever apprehends it should deliver it to me immediately and without delay. Judge for yourself. How, indeed, can I do without such a conspicuous part of my body? It isn't like some little toe which I put into my boot, and no one can see whether it is there or not. On Thursdays I call at the house of Mrs. Chekhtaryova, a state councillor's wife. Mrs. Podtochina, Pelageya Grigoryevna, a field officer's wife, and her very pretty daughter, are also very good friends of mine, and you can judge for yourself how can I now . . . I can't appear at their house now."

The clerk thought hard, his lips pursed tightly in witness thereof.

"No, I can't insert such an advertisement in the papers," he said at last after a long silence.

"How so? Why?"

"Well, the paper might lose its reputation. If everyone were to write that his nose had run away, why . . . As it is, people say that too many absurd stories and false rumors are printed."

"But why is this business absurd? I don't think it is anything of the sort."

"That's what you think. But take last week, there was another such case. A civil servant came in, just as you have, bringing a note, was billed two rubles seventy-three kopecks, and all the advertisement consisted of was that a black-coated poodle had run away. Doesn't seem to amount to much, does it now? But it turned out to be a libel. This so-called poodle was the treasurer of I don't recall what institution."

"But I am not putting in an advertisement about a poodle—it's about my very own nose; that is, practically the same as about myself."

"No, I can't possibly insert such an advertisement."

"But when my nose actually has disappeared!"

"If it has disappeared, then it's a doctor's business. They say there are people who can fix you up with any nose you like. However, I observe that you must be a man of gay disposition and fond of kidding in company."

"I swear to you by all that is holy! Perhaps, if it comes to that, why I'll show you."

"Why trouble yourself?" continued the clerk, taking a pinch of snuff. "However, if it isn't too much trouble," he added, moved by curiosity, "I'd like to have a look."

The collegiate assessor removed the handkerchief from his face.

"Very strange indeed!" said the clerk. "It's absolutely flat, like a pancake fresh off the griddle. Yes, incredibly smooth."

"Well, will you go on arguing after this? You see yourself that you can't refuse to print my advertisement. I'll be particularly grateful and am very glad that this opportunity has given me the pleasure of making your acquaintance. . . ." The major, as we can see, decided this time to use a little flattery.

"To insert it would be easy enough, of course," said the clerk, "but I don't see any advantage to you in it. If you really must, give it to someone who wields a skillful pen and let him describe this as a rare phenomenon of nature and publish this little item in *The Northern Bee*" (here he took another pinch of snuff) "for the benefit of the young" (here he wiped his nose), "or just so, as a matter of general interest."

The collegiate assessor felt completely discouraged. He dropped his eyes to the lower part of the paper where theatrical performances were announced. His face was about to break out into a smile as he came across the name of a pretty actress, and his hand went to his pocket to check whether he had a blue note, because in his opinion field officers ought to sit in the stalls—but the thought of his nose spoiled it all.

The clerk himself seemed to be moved by Kovalyov's embarrassing situation. Wishing at least to ease his distress he deemed it appropriate to express his sympathy in a few words: "I really am grieved that such a thing happened to you. Wouldn't you care for a pinch of snuff? It dispels headaches and melancholy; it's even good for hemorrhoids." With those words the clerk offered Kovalyov his snuff-box, rather deftly snapping open the lid which pictured a lady in a hat.

This unpremeditated action made Kovalyov lose all patience. "I can't understand how you find this a time for jokes," he said angrily. "Can't you see that I lack the very thing one needs to take snuff? To hell with your snuff! I can't bear the sight of it now, even if you offered me some *râpé* itself, let alone your wretched Berezin's." After saying this he left the newspaper office, deeply vexed, and went to visit the district police inspector, a man with a passion for sugar. In his house the entire parlor, which served also as the dining room, was stacked with sugar loaves which local tradesmen brought to him out of friendship. At the moment his cook was pulling off the inspector's regulation topboots; his sword and all his military trappings were already hanging peacefully in the corners, and his three-year-old son was reaching for his redoubtable three-cornered hat, while the inspector himself was preparing to taste the fruits of peace after his day of warlike, martial pursuits.

Kovalyov came in at the moment when the inspector had just stretched, grunted and said, "Oh, for a couple of hours' good snooze!" It was therefore easy to see that the collegiate assessor had come at quite the wrong time. And I wonder whether he would have been welcome even if he had brought several pounds of tea or a piece of cloth. The police inspector was a great patron of all arts and manufactures, but he preferred a bank note to everything else. "This is the thing," he would usually say. "There can be nothing better than it—it doesn't ask for food, it doesn't take much space, it'll always fit into a pocket, and if you drop it it won't break."

The inspector received Kovalyov rather coolly and said that after dinner was hardly the time to conduct investigations, that nature itself intended that man should rest a little after a good meal (from this the collegiate assessor could see that the aphorisms of the ancient sages were not unknown to the police inspector), that no real gentleman would allow his nose to be pulled off, and that there were many majors in this world who hadn't even decent underwear and hung about in all sorts of disreputable places.

This last was too close for comfort. It must be observed that Kovalyov was extremely quick to take offense. He could forgive whatever was said about himself, but never anything that referred to rank or title. He was even of the opinion that in plays one could allow references to junior officers, but that there should be no criticism of field officers. His reception by the inspector so disconcerted him that he tossed his head and said with an air of dignity, spreading his arms slightly: "I confess that after such offensive remarks on your part, I've nothing more to add. . . ." and left the room.

He came home hardly able to stand on his feet. It was already dusk. After all this fruitless search his apartment appeared to him melancholy or extraordinarily squalid. Coming into the entrance hall he caught sight of his valet Ivan who, lying on his back on the soiled leather sofa, was spitting at the ceiling and rather successfully hitting one and the same spot. Such indifference on the man's part infuriated him; he struck him on the forehead with his hat, saying, "You pig, always doing something stupid!"

Ivan jumped up abruptly and rushed to take off his cloak.

Entering his room the major, tired and sad, sank into an armchair and at last, after several sighs, said:

"O Lord, O Lord! What have I done to deserve such misery? Had I lost an arm or a leg, it would not have been so bad; had I lost my ears, it would have been bad enough but nevertheless bearable; but without a nose a man is goodness knows what; he's not a bird, he's not a human being; in fact, just take him and throw him out the window! And if at least it had been chopped off in battle or in a duel, or if I myself had been to blame; but it disappeared just like that, with nothing, nothing at all to show for it. But no, it can't be," he added after some thought. "It's unbelievable that a nose should disappear; absolutely unbelievable. I must be either dreaming or just imagining it. Maybe, somehow, by mistake instead of water I drank the vodka which I rub on my chin after shaving. That fool Ivan didn't take it away and I probably gulped it down."—To satisfy himself that he was not drunk the major pinched himself so hard that he cried out. The pain he felt fully convinced him that he was wide awake. He stealthily approached the mirror and at first half-closed his eyes, thinking that perhaps the nose would appear in its proper place; but the same moment he sprang back exclaiming, "What a caricature of a face!"

It was indeed incomprehensible. If a button, a silver spoon, a watch, or some such thing had disappeared—but to disappear, and for whom to disappear? and besides in his own apartment, too! . . . After considering all the circumstances, Major Kovalyov was inclined to think that most likely it was the fault of none other than the field officer's wife, Mrs. Podtochina, who wanted him to marry her daughter. He, too, liked to flirt with her but avoided a final showdown. And when the field officer's wife told him point-blank that she wanted to marry her daughter off to him, he eased off on his attentions, saying that he was still young, that he had to serve another five years when he would be exactly forty-two. And so the field officer's wife, presumably in revenge, had decided to put a curse on him and hired for this purpose some old witchwomen, because it was impossible even to suppose that the nose had been simply cut off: no one had entered his room; the barber, Ivan Yakovlevich, had shaved him as recently as Wednesday and throughout that whole day and even on Thursday his nose was all there—he remembered and knew it very well. Besides, he would have felt the pain and no doubt the wound could not have healed so soon and be as smooth as a pancake. Different plans of action occurred to him: should he formally summons Mrs. Podtochina to court or go to her himself and expose her in person? His reflections were interrupted by light breaking through all the cracks in the door, which told him that Ivan had lit the candle in the hall. Soon Ivan himself appeared, carrying it before him and brightly illuminating the whole room. Kovalyov's first gesture was to snatch his handkerchief and cover the place where his nose had been only the day before, so that indeed the silly fellow would not stand there gaping at such an oddity in his master's strange appearance.

Barely had Ivan gone into his cubbyhole when an unfamiliar voice was heard in the hall saying, "Does Collegiate Assessor Kovalyov live here?"

"Come in. Major Kovalyov is here," said Kovalyov, jumping up quickly and opening the door.

In came a police officer of handsome appearance with sidewhiskers that were neither too light nor too dark, and rather full cheeks, the very same who at the beginning of this story was standing at the end of St. Isaac's Bridge.

"Did you happen to mislay your nose?"

"That's right."

"It has been recovered."

"What are you saying!" exclaimed Major Kovalyov. He was tongue-tied with joy. He stared at the police officer standing in front of him, on whose full lips and cheeks the trembling light of the candle flickered. "How?"

"By an odd piece of luck—he was intercepted on the point of leaving town. He was about to board a stagecoach and leave for Riga. He even had a passport made out a long time ago in the name of a certain civil servant. Strangely enough, I also at first took him for a gentleman. But fortunately I had my glasses with me and I saw at once that it was a nose. You see, I am nearsighted and when you stand before me all I can see is that you have a face, but I can't make out if you have a nose or a beard or anything. My mother-in-law, that is, my wife's mother, can't see anything, either."

Kovalyov was beside himself. "Where is it? Where? I'll run there at once."

"Don't trouble yourself. Knowing that you need it I have brought it with me. And the strange thing is that the chief villain in this business is that rascally barber from Voznesensky Street who is now in a lockup. I have long suspected him of drunkenness and theft, and as recently as the day before yesterday he stole a dozen buttons from a certain shop. Your nose is quite in order."—With these words the police officer reached into his pocket and pulled out a nose wrapped up in a piece of paper.

"That's it!" shouted Kovalyov. "That's it, all right! Do join me in a little cup of tea today."

"I would consider it a great pleasure, but I simply can't: I have to drop in at a mental asylum. . . . All food prices have gone up enormously. . . . I have my mother-in-law, that's my wife's mother, living with me, and my children; the eldest is particularly promising, a very clever lad, but we haven't the means to educate him."

Kovalyov grasped his meaning and, snatching up a red banknote from the table, thrust it into the hands of the inspector who, clicking his heels, went out the door. Almost the very same instant Kovalyov heard his voice out in the street where he was admonishing with his fist a stupid peasant who had driven his cart onto the boulevard.

After the police officer had left, the collegiate assessor remained for a few minutes in a sort of indefinable state and only after several minutes recovered the capacity to see and feel: his unexpected joy had made him lose his senses. He carefully took the newly found nose in both his cupped hands and once again examined it thoroughly.

"That's it, that's it, all right," said Major Kovalyov. "Here on the left side is the pimple which swelled up yesterday." The major very nearly laughed with joy.

But there is nothing enduring in this world, and that is why even joy is not as keen in the moment that follows the first; and a moment later it grows weaker still and finally merges imperceptibly into one's usual state of mind, just as a ring on the water, made by the fall of a pebble, merges finally into the smooth surface. Kovalyov began to reflect and realized that the whole business was not yet over: the nose was found but it still had to be affixed, put in its proper place.

"And what if it doesn't stick?"

At this question, addressed to himself, the major turned pale.

Seized by unaccountable fear, he rushed to the table and drew the looking-glass closer, to avoid affixing the nose crookedly. His hands trembled. Carefully and deliberately, he put it in its former place. O horror! the nose wouldn't stick. . . . He carried it to his mouth, warmed it slightly with his breath, and again brought it to the smooth place between his two cheeks; but the nose just wouldn't stay on.

"Well, come on, come on, you fool!" he kept saying to it. But the nose was as though made of wood and plopped back on the table with a strange corklike sound. The major's face was twisted in convulsion. "Won't it really grow on?" he said fearfully. But no matter how many times he tried to fit it in its proper place, his efforts were unsuccessful as before.

He called Ivan and sent him for the doctor who occupied the best apartment on the first floor of the same house. The doctor was a fine figure of a man; he had beautiful pitch-black sidewhiskers, a fresh, healthy wife, ate raw apples first thing in the morning, and kept his mouth extraordinarily clean, rinsing it every morning for nearly three quarters of an hour and polishing his teeth with five different kinds of little brushes. The doctor came at once. After asking him how long ago the mishap had occurred, he lifted Major Kovalyov's face by the chin and flicked him with his thumb on the very spot where the nose used to be, so that the major had to throw his head back with such force that he hit the back of it against the wall. The doctor said this didn't matter and, suggesting that he move a little away from the wall, told him first to bend his head to the right, and, after feeling the spot where the nose had been, said "Hmm!" Then he told him to bend his head to the left and said "Hmm!"; and in conclusion he again flicked him with his thumb so that Major Kovalyov jerked his head like a horse whose teeth are being examined. Having carried out this test, the doctor shook his head and said: "No, can't be done. You'd better stay like this, or we might make things even worse. Of course, it can be stuck on. I daresay, I could do it right now for you, but I assure you it'll be worse for you."

"I like that! How am I to remain without a nose?" said Kovalyov. "It couldn't possibly be worse than now. This is simply a hell of a thing! How can I show myself anywhere in such a scandalous state? I have acquaintances in good society; why, this evening, now, I am expected at parties in two houses. I know many people: Mrs. Chekhtaryova, a state councillor's wife, Mrs. Podtochina, a field officer's wife . . . although after what she's done now I'll have nothing more to do with her except through the police. I appeal to you," pleaded Kovalyov, "is there no way at all? Fix it on somehow, even if not very well, just so it stays on; in an emergency, I could even prop it up with my hand. And besides, I don't dance, so I can't do any harm by some careless movement. As regards my grateful acknowledgment of your visits, be assured that as far as my means allow . . . ."

"Would you believe it," said the doctor in a voice that was neither loud nor soft but extremely persuasive and magnetic, "I never treat people out of self-interest. This is against my principles and my calling. It is true that I charge for my visits, but solely in order not to offend by my refusal. Of course I could affix your nose; but I assure you on my honor, if you won't take my word for it, that it will be much worse. Rather, let nature take its course. Wash the place more often with cold water, and I assure you that without a nose you'll be as healthy as if you had one. As for the nose itself, I advise you to put the nose in a jar with alcohol, or, better still, pour into the jar two tablespoonfuls of aqua fortis and warmed-up vinegar—and then you can get good money for it. I'll buy it myself, if you don't ask too much."

"No, no! I won't sell it for anything!" exclaimed Major Kovalyov in desperation. "Let it rather go to blazes!"

"Excuse me!" said the doctor, bowing himself out, "I wanted to be of some use to you. . . . Never mind! At least you saw my good will." Having said this the doctor left the room with a dignified air. Kovalyov didn't even notice his face and in his benumbed state saw nothing but the cuffs of his snow-white shirt peeping out of the sleeves of his black tailcoat.

The very next day he decided, before lodging a complaint, to write to Mrs. Podtochina requesting her to restore him his due without a fight. The letter ran as follows:

Dear Madam Alexandra * Grigoryevna,

I fail to understand your strange behavior. Be assured that, acting in this way, you gain nothing and certainly will not force me to marry your daughter. Believe me that the incident with my nose is fully known to me, just as is the fact that you—and no one else—are the principal person involved. Its sudden detachment from its place, its flight and its disguise, first as a certain civil servant, then at last in its own shape, is nothing other than the result of a spell cast by you or by those who engage like you in such noble pursuits. I for my part deem it my duty to forewarn you that if the abovementioned nose is not back in its place this very day I shall be forced to resort to the defense and protection of the law.

Whereupon I have the honor to remain, with my full respect,

Your obedient servant
Platon Kovalyov

Dear Sir
Platon Kuzmich,

Your letter came as a complete surprise to me. I frankly confess that I never expected it, especially as regards your unjust reproaches. I beg to inform you that I never received in my house the civil servant you mention, neither in disguise nor in his actual shape. It is true that Filipp Ivanovich Potanchikov had been visiting me. And though he did indeed seek my daughter's hand, being himself of good sober conduct and great learning, I never held out any hopes to him. You also mention your nose. If by this you mean that I wanted to put your nose out of joint, that is, to give you a formal refusal, then I am surprised to hear you mention it, for I, as you know, was of the exactly opposite opinion, and if you now seek my daughter in marriage in the lawful way, I am ready to give you immediate satisfaction, for this has always been the object of my keenest desire, in the hope of which I remain always at your service,

Alexandra Podtochina

"No," said Kovalyov, after he had read the letter. "She certainly isn't guilty. Impossible! The letter is written in a way no person guilty of a crime can write."—The collegiate assessor was an expert in this matter, having been sent several times to take part in a judicial investigation while still serving in the Caucasus.—"How then, how on earth could this have happened? The devil alone can make it out," he said at last in utter dejection.

* [Earlier in the story her first name is Pelageya.—EDITOR, 1992.]

In the meantime rumors about this extraordinary occurrence had spread all over the capital and, as is usual in such cases, not without some special accretions. In those days the minds of everybody were particularly inclined toward things extraordinary: not long before, the whole town had shown an interest in experiments with the effects of hypnotism. Moreover, the story of the dancing chairs in Konyushen-naya Street was still fresh in memory, and one should not be surprised therefore that soon people began saying that Collegiate Assessor Ko-valyov's nose went strolling along Nevsky Avenue at precisely three o'clock. Throngs of curious people came there every day. Someone said that the Nose was in Junker's store: and such a crowd and jam was created outside Junker's that the police had to intervene. One profit-seeker of respectable appearance, with sidewhiskers, who sold a variety of dry pastries at the entrance to a theater, had specially constructed excellent, sturdy wooden benches, on which he invited the curious to mount for eighty kopecks apiece. One veteran colonel made a point of leaving his house earlier than usual and with much difficulty made his way through the crowd, but to his great indignation saw in the window of the shop instead of the nose an ordinary woollen undershirt and a lithograph showing a young girl straightening her stocking and a dandy, with a lapeled waistcoat and a small beard, peeping at her from behind a tree—a picture which had been hanging in the same place for more than ten years. Moving away he said with annoyance, "How can they confound the people by such silly and unlikely rumors?"—Then a rumor went round that Major Kovalyov's nose was out for a stroll, not on Nevsky Avenue but in Taurida Gardens, that it had been there for ages; that when Khosrev-Mirza lived there he marveled greatly at this strange freak of nature. Some students from the Surgical Academy went there. One aristocratic, respectable lady, in a special letter to the Super-intendent of the Gardens, asked him to show her children this rare phenomenon, accompanied, if possible, with an explanation edifying and instructive for the young.

All the men about town, the *habitués* of society parties, who liked to amuse ladies and whose resources had by that time been exhausted, were extremely glad of all these goings-on. A small percentage of respectable and well-meaning people were extremely displeased. One gentleman said indignantly that he could not understand how in this enlightened age such senseless stories could spread and that he was surprised at the government's failure to take heed of it. This gentleman apparently was one of those gentlemen who would like to embroil the government in everything, even in their daily quarrels with their wives. After that . . . but here again the whole incident is shrouded in fog, and what happened afterwards is absolutely unknown.

III

UTTERLY NONSENSICAL things happen in this world. Sometimes there is absolutely no rhyme or reason in them: suddenly the very nose which had been going around with the rank of a state councillor and created such a stir in the city, found itself again, as though nothing were the matter, in its proper place, that is to say, between the two cheeks of Major Kovalyov. This happened on April 7th. Waking up and chancing to look in the mirror, he sees—his nose! He grabbed it with his hand—his nose indeed! "Aha!" said Kovalyov, and in his joy he very nearly broke into a barefooted dance round the room, but Ivan's entry stopped him. He told Ivan to bring him some water to wash in and, while washing, glanced again at the mirror—his nose! Drying himself with his towel, he again glanced at the mirror—his nose!

"Take a look, Ivan, I think there's a pimple on my nose," he said, and in the meantime thought, "How awful if Ivan says: 'Why, no sir, not only there is no pimple but also the nose itself is gone!' "

But Ivan said: "Nothing, sir, no pimple—your nose is fine!"

"That's great, damn it!" the major said to himself, snapping his fingers. At that moment the barber Ivan Yakovlevich peeped in at the door but as timidly as a cat which had just been whipped for stealing lard.

"First you tell me—are your hands clean?" Kovalyov shouted to him before he had approached.

"They are."

"You're lying."

"I swear they are, sir."

"Well, we'll see."

Kovalyov sat down. Ivan Yakovlevich draped him with a napkin and instantly, with the help of a shaving brush, transformed his chin and part of his cheek into the whipped cream served at merchants' namesday parties. "Well, I never!" Ivan Yakovlevich said to himself, glancing at his nose, and then cocked his head on the other side and looked at it sideways: "Look at that! Just you try and figure that out," he continued and took a good look at his nose. At last, gently, with the greatest care imaginable, he raised two fingers to grasp it by the tip. Such was Ivan Yakovlevich's method.

"Now, now, now, look out there!" cried Kovalyov. Dumbfounded and confused as never before in his life, Ivan Yakovlevich let his hands drop. At last he began cautiously tickling him with the razor under the chin, and although it wasn't at all handy for him and difficult to shave without holding on to the olfactory portion of the face, nevertheless, somehow bracing his gnarled thumb against the cheek and the lower jaw, he finally overcame all obstacles and finished shaving him.

When everything was ready, Kovalyov hastened to dress, hired a cab and went straight to the coffee-house. Before he was properly inside the door he shouted, "Boy, a cup of chocolate!" and immediately made for the mirror: the nose was there. He turned round cheerfully and looked ironically, slightly screwing up one eye, at two military gentlemen one of whom had a nose no bigger than a waistcoat button. After that he set off for the office of the department where he was trying to obtain the post of a vice-governor or, failing that, of a procurement officer. Passing through the reception room, he glanced in the mirror: the nose was there. Then he went to visit another collegiate assessor or major, a great wag, to whom he often said in reply to various derisive remarks: "Oh, come off it, I know you, you're a kidder." On the way there he thought: "If the major doesn't explode with laughter on seeing me, it's a sure sign that everything is in its proper place." The collegiate assessor did not explode. "That's great, that's great, damn it!" Kovalyov thought to himself. On the street he met Mrs. Podtochina, the field officer's wife, together with her daughter, bowed to them and was hailed with joyful exclamations, and so everything was all right, no part of him was missing. He talked with them a very long time and, deliberately taking out his snuff-box, right in front of them kept stuffing his nose with snuff at both entrances for a very long time, saying to himself: "So much for you, you women, you stupid hens! I won't marry the daughter all the same. Anything else, *par amour*—by all means." And from that time on, Major Kovalyov went strolling about as though nothing had happened, both on Nevsky Avenue, and in the theaters, and everywhere. And his nose too, as though nothing had happened, stayed on his face, betraying no sign of having played truant. And thereafter Major Kovalyov was always seen in good humor, smiling, running after absolutely all the pretty ladies, and once even stopping in front of a little shop in Gostinny Dvor and buying himself the ribbon of some order, goodness knows why, for he hadn't been decorated with any order.

That is the kind of affair that happened in the northern capital of our vast empire. Only now, on second thoughts, can we see that there is much that is improbable in it. Without speaking of the fact that the supernatural detachment of the nose and its appearance in various places in the guise of a state councillor is indeed strange, how is it that Kovalyov did not realize that one does not advertise for one's nose through the newspaper office? I do not mean to say that advertising rates appear to me too high: that's nonsense, and I am not at all one of those mercenary people. But it's improper, embarrassing, not nice! And then again—how did the nose come to be in a newly baked loaf, and how about Ivan Yakovlevich? . . . No, this is something I can't understand, positively can't understand. But the strangest, the most incomprehensible thing of all, is how authors can choose such subjects. I confess that this is quite inconceivable; it is indeed . . . no, no, I just can't understand it at all! In the first place, there is absolutely no benefit in it for the fatherland; in the second place . . . but in the second place, there is no benefit either. I simply don't know what to make of it. . . .

And yet, in spite of it all, though, of course, we may assume this and that and the other, perhaps even . . . And after all, where aren't there incongruities?—But all the same, when you think about it, there really is something in all this. Whatever anyone says, such things happen in this world; rarely, but they do.

The Overcoat

IN THE DEPARTMENT OF . . . but it is better not to name the department. There is nothing more irritable than all kinds of departments, regiments, courts of justice and, in a word, every branch of public service. Each separate man nowadays thinks all society insulted in his person. They say that, quite recently, a complaint was received from a justice of the peace, in which he plainly demonstrated that all the imperial institutions were going to the dogs, and that his sacred name was being taken in vain; and in proof he appended to the complaint a huge volume of some romantic composition, in which the justice of the peace appears about once in every ten lines, sometimes in a drunken condition. Therefore, in order to avoid all unpleasantness, it will be better for us to designate the department in question as *a certain department*.

So, *in a certain department* serves *a certain official*—not a very prominent official, it must be allowed—short of stature, somewhat pock-marked, rather red-haired, rather blind, judging from appearances, with a small bald spot on his forehead, with wrinkles on his cheeks, with a complexion of the sort called sanguine. . . . How could he help it? The Petersburg climate was responsible for that. As for his rank—for with us the rank must be stated first of all—he was what is called a perpetual titular councillor, over which, as is well known, some writers make merry and crack their jokes, as they have the praiseworthy custom of attacking those who cannot bite back.

His family name was Bashmachkin. It is evident from the name, that it originated in *bashmak* (shoe); but when, at what time, and in what manner, is not known. His father and grandfather, and even his brother-in-law, and all the Bashmachkins, always wore boots, and only had new

79

heels two or three times a year. His name was Akakii Akakievich. It may strike the reader as rather singular and far-fetched; but he may feel assured that it was by no means far-fetched, and that the circumstances were such that it would have been impossible to give him any other name; and this was how it came about.

Akakii Akakievich was born, if my memory fails me not, towards night on the 23d of March. His late mother, the wife of an official, and a very fine woman, made all due arrangements for having the child baptized. His mother was lying on the bed opposite the door: on her right stood the godfather, a most estimable man, Ivan Ivanovich Eroshkin, who served as presiding officer of the senate; and the godmother, the wife of an officer of the quarter, a woman of rare virtues, Anna Semenovna Byelobrush-kova. They offered the mother her choice of three names—Mokiya, Sossiya or that the child should be called after the martyr Khozdazat. "No," pronounced the blessed woman, "all those names are poor." In order to please her, they opened the calendar at another place: three more names appeared—Triphilii, Dula and Varakhasii. "This is a judgment," said the old woman. "What names! I truly never heard the like. Varadat or Varukh might have been borne, but not Triphilii and Varakhasii!" They turned another page—Pavsikakhii and Vakhtisii. "Now I see," said the old woman, "that it is plainly fate. And if that's the case, it will be better to name him after his father. His father's name was Akakii, so let his son's be also Akakii." In this manner he became Akakii Akakievich.

They christened the child, whereat he wept, and made a grimace, as though he foresaw that he was to be a titular councillor. In this manner did it all come about. We have mentioned it, in order that the reader might see for himself that it happened quite as a case of necessity, and that it was utterly impossible to give him any other name. When and how he entered the department, and who appointed him, no one could remember. However much the directors and chiefs of all kinds were changed, he was always to be seen in the same place, the same attitude, the same occupation—the same official for letters; so that afterwards it was affirmed that he had been born in undress uniform with a bald spot on his head.

No respect was shown him in the department. The janitor not only did not rise from his seat when he passed, but never even glanced at him, as if only a fly had flown through the reception-room. His superiors treated him in a coolly despotic manner. Some assistant chief would thrust a paper under his nose without so much as saying, "Copy," or, "Here's a nice, interesting matter," or any thing else agreeable, as is customary in well-bred service. And he took it, looking only at the paper, and not observing who handed it to him, or whether he had the right to do so: he simply took it, and set about copying it.

The young officials laughed at and made fun of him, so far as their official wit permitted; recounted there in his presence various stories concocted about him, and about his landlady, an old woman of seventy; they said that she beat him; asked when the wedding was to be; and strewed bits of paper over his head, calling them snow. But Akakii Akakievich answered not a word, as though there had been no one before him. It even had no effect upon his employment: amid all these molestations he never made a single mistake in a letter.

But if the joking became utterly intolerable, as when they jogged his hand, and prevented his attending to his work, he would exclaim, "Leave me alone! Why do you insult me?" And there was something strange in the words and the voice in which they were uttered. There was in it a something which moved to pity; so that one young man, lately entered, who, taking pattern by the others, had permitted himself to make sport of him, suddenly stopped short, as though all had undergone a transformation before him, and presented itself in a different aspect. Some unseen force repelled him from the comrades whose acquaintance he had made, on the supposition that they were well-bred and polite men. And long afterwards, in his gayest moments, there came to his mind the little official with the bald forehead, with the heart-rending words, "Leave me alone! Why do you insult me?" And in these penetrating words, other words resounded—"I am thy brother." And the poor young man covered his face with his hand; and many a time afterwards, in the course of his life, he shuddered at seeing how much inhumanity there is in man, how much savage coarseness is concealed in delicate, refined worldliness and, O God! even in that man whom the world acknowledges as honorable and noble.

It would be difficult to find another man who lived so entirely for his duties. It is saying but little to say that he served with zeal: no, he served with love. In that copying, he saw a varied and agreeable world. Enjoyment was written on his face: some letters were favorites with him; and when he encountered them, he became unlike himself; he smiled and winked, and assisted with his lips, so that it seemed as though each letter might be read in his face, as his pen traced it. If his pay had been in proportion to his zeal, he would, perhaps, to his own surprise, have been made even a councillor of state. But he served, as his companions, the wits, put it, like a buckle in a button-hole.

Moreover, it is impossible to say that no attention was paid to him. One director being a kindly man, and desirous of rewarding him for his long service, ordered him to be given something more important than mere copying; namely, he was ordered to make a report of an already concluded affair, to another court: the matter consisted simply in changing the heading, and altering a few words from the first to the third person. This caused him so much toil, that he was all in a perspiration, rubbed his forehead, and finally said, "No, give me rather something to copy." After that they let him copy on forever.

Outside this copying, it appeared that nothing existed for him. He thought not at all of his clothes: his undress uniform was not green, but a sort of rusty-meal color. The collar was narrow, low, so that his neck, in spite of the fact that it was not long, seemed inordinately long as it emerged from that collar, like the necks of plaster cats which wag their heads, and are carried about upon the heads of scores of Russian foreigners. And something was always sticking to his uniform—either a piece of hay or some trifle. Moreover, he had a peculiar knack, as he walked in the street, of arriving beneath a window when all sorts of rubbish was being flung out of it: hence he always bore about on his hat melon and watermelon rinds, and other such stuff.

Never once in his life did he give heed to what was going on every day in the street; while it is well known that his young brother official, extending the range of his bold glance, gets so that he can see when any one's trouser-straps drop down upon the opposite sidewalk, which always calls forth a malicious smile upon his face. But Akakii Akakievich, if he looked at anything, saw in all things the clean, even strokes of his written lines; and only when a horse thrust his muzzle, from some unknown quarter, over his shoulder, and sent a whole gust of wind down his neck from his nostrils, did he observe that he was not in the middle of a line, but in the middle of the street.

On arriving at home, he sat down at once at the table, supped his cabbage-soup quickly and ate a bit of beef with onions, never noticing their taste, ate it all with flies and anything else which the Lord sent at the moment. On observing that his stomach began to puff out, he rose from the table, took out a little vial with ink and copied papers which he had brought home. If there happened to be none, he took copies for himself, for his own gratification, especially if the paper was noteworthy, not on account of its beautiful style, but of its being addressed to some new or distinguished person.

Even at the hour when the gray Petersburg sky had quite disappeared, and all the world of officials had eaten or dined, each as he could, in accordance with the salary he received, and his own fancy; when all were resting from the departmental jar of pens, running to and fro, their own and other people's indispensable occupations and all the work that an uneasy man makes willingly for himself, rather than what is necessary; when officials hasten to dedicate to pleasure the time that is left to them—one bolder than the rest goes to the theater; another, into the streets, devoting it to the inspection of some bonnets; one wastes his evening in compliments to some pretty girl, the star of a small official circle; one—and this is the most common case of all—goes to his comrades on the fourth or third floor, to two small rooms with an ante-room or kitchen, and some pretensions to fashion, a lamp or some other trifle which has cost many a sacrifice of dinner or excursion—in a word, even at the hour when all officials disperse among the contracted quarters of their friends, to play at whist, as they sip their tea from glasses with a kopek's worth of sugar, draw smoke through long pipes, relating at times some bits of gossip which a Russian man can never, under any circumstances, refrain from, or even when there is nothing to say, recounting everlasting anecdotes about the commandant whom they had sent to inform that the tail of the horse on the Falconet Monument* had been cut off—in a word, even when all strive to divert themselves, Akakii Akakievich yielded to no diversion.

No one could ever say that he had seen him at any sort of an evening party. Having written to his heart's content, he lay down to sleep, smiling at the thought of the coming day—of what God might send to copy on the morrow. Thus flowed on the peaceful life of the man, who, with a salary of four hundred rubles, understood how to be content with his fate; and thus it would have continued to flow on, perhaps, to extreme old age, were there not various ills sown among the path of life for titular councillors as well as for private, actual, court and every other species of councillor, even for those who never give any advice or take any themselves.

There exists in Petersburg a powerful foe of all who receive four hundred rubles salary a year, or thereabouts. This foe is no other than our Northern cold, although it is said to be very wholesome. At nine o'clock in the morning, at the very hour when the streets are filled with men bound for the departments, it begins to bestow such powerful and piercing nips on all noses impartially that the poor officials really do not know what to do with them. At the hour when the foreheads of even those who occupy exalted positions ache with the cold, and tears start to their eyes, the poor titular councillors are sometimes unprotected. Their only salvation lies in traversing as quickly as possible, in their thin little overcoats, five or six streets, and then warming their feet well in the porter's room, and so thawing all their talents and qualifications for official service, which had become frozen on the way.

Akakii Akakievich had felt for some time that his back and shoulders suffered with peculiar poignancy, in spite of the fact that he tried to traverse the legal distance with all possible speed. He finally wondered whether the fault did not lie in his overcoat. He examined it thoroughly at home, and discovered that in two places, namely, on the back and shoulders, it had become thin as mosquito-netting: the cloth was worn to such a degree that he could see through it, and the lining had fallen into pieces.

* [The famous equestrian statue of Peter the Great, the work of the French sculptor Etienne-Maurice Falconet, 1716–1791.—EDITOR, 1992.]

You must know that Akakii Akakievich's overcoat served as an object of ridicule to the officials: they even deprived it of the noble name of overcoat, and called it a kapota.* In fact, it was of singular make: its collar diminished year by year, but served to patch its other parts. The patching did not exhibit great skill on the part of the tailor, and turned out, in fact, baggy and ugly. Seeing how the matter stood, Akakii Akakievich decided that it would be necessary to take the overcoat to Petrovich, the tailor, who lived somewhere on the fourth floor up a dark staircase, and who, in spite of his having but one eye, and pock-marks all over his face, busied himself with considerable success in repairing the trousers and coats of officials and others; that is to say, when he was sober, and not nursing some other scheme in his head.

It is not necessary to say much about this tailor: but, as it is the custom to have the character of each personage in a novel clearly defined, there is nothing to be done; so here is Petrovich the tailor. At first he was called only Grigorii, and was some gentleman's serf: he began to call himself Petrovich from the time when he received his free papers, and began to drink heavily on all holidays, at first on the great ones, and then on all church festivals without discrimination, wherever a cross stood in the calendar. On this point he was faithful to ancestral custom; and, quarrelling with his wife, he called her a low female and a German.

As we have stumbled upon his wife, it will be necessary to say a word or two about her; but, unfortunately, little is known of her beyond the fact that Petrovich has a wife, who wears a cap and a dress; but she cannot lay claim to beauty, it seems—at least, no one but the soldiers of the guard, as they pulled their mustaches, and uttered some peculiar sound, even looked under her cap when they met her.

Ascending the staircase which led to Petrovich—which, to do it justice, was all soaked in water (dishwater), and penetrated with the smell of spirits which affects the eyes, and is an inevitable adjunct to all dark stairways in Petersburg houses—ascending the stairs, Akakii Akakievich pondered how much Petrovich would ask, and mentally resolved not to give more than two rubles. The door was open; for the mistress, in cooking some fish, had raised such a smoke in the kitchen that not even the beetles were visible.

Akakii Akakievich passed through the kitchen unperceived, even by the housewife, and at length reached a room where he beheld Petrovich seated on a large, unpainted table, with his legs tucked under him like a Turkish pasha. His feet were bare, after the fashion of tailors as they sit at work; and the first thing which arrested the eye was his thumb, very well known to Akakii Akakievich, with a deformed nail thick and strong as a

* A woman's cloak.—TRANSLATOR.

turtle's shell. On Petrovich's neck hung a skein of silk and thread, and upon his knees lay some old garment. He had been trying for three minutes to thread his needle, unsuccessfully, and so was very angry with the darkness, and even with the thread, growling in a low voice, "It won't go through, the barbarian! you pricked me, you rascal!"

Akakii Akakievich was displeased at arriving at the precise moment when Petrovich was angry: he liked to order something of Petrovich when the latter was a little downhearted, or, as his wife expressed it, "when he had settled himself with brandy, the one-eyed devil!" Under such circumstances, Petrovich generally came down in his price very readily, and came to an understanding, and even bowed and returned thanks. Afterwards, to be sure, his wife came, complaining that her husband was drunk, and so had set the price too low; but, if only a ten-kopek piece were added, then the matter was settled. But now it appeared that Petrovich was in a sober condition, and therefore rough, taciturn, and inclined to demand, Satan only knows what price. Akakii Akakievich felt this, and would gladly have beat a retreat, as the saying goes; but he was in for it. Petrovich screwed up his one eye very intently at him; and Akakii Akakievich involuntarily said, "How do you do, Petrovich!"

"I wish you a good-morning, sir," said Petrovich, and squinted at Akakii Akakievich's hands, wishing to see what sort of booty he had brought.

"Ah! I . . . to you, Petrovich, this"—It must be known that Akakii Akakievich expressed himself chiefly by prepositions, adverbs, and by such scraps of phrases as had no meaning whatever. But if the matter was a very difficult one, then he had a habit of never completing his sentences; so that quite frequently, having begun his phrase with the words, "This, in fact, is quite" . . . there was no more of it, and he forgot himself, thinking that he had already finished it.

"What is it?" asked Petrovich, and with his one eye scanned his whole uniform, beginning with the collar down to the cuffs, the back, the tails and button-holes, all of which were very well known to him, because they were his own handiwork. Such is the habit of tailors: it is the first thing they do on meeting one.

"But I, here, this, Petrovich, . . . an overcoat, cloth . . . here you see, everywhere, in different places, it is quite strong . . . it is a little dusty, and looks old, but it is new, only here in one place it is a little . . . on the back, and here on one of the shoulders, it is a little worn, yes, here on this shoulder it is a little . . . do you see? this is all. And a little work" . . .

Petrovich took the overcoat, spread it out, to begin with, on the table, looked long at it, shook his head, put out his hand to the window-sill after his snuff-box, adorned with the portrait of some general—just what general is unknown, for the place where the face belonged had been rubbed through by the finger, and a square bit of paper had been pasted on. Having taken a pinch of snuff, Petrovich spread the overcoat out on his hands, and inspected it against the light, and again shook his head; then he turned it, lining upwards, and shook his head once more; again he removed the general-adorned cover with its bit of pasted paper, and, having stuffed his nose with snuff, covered and put away the snuff-box, and said finally, "No, it is impossible to mend it: it's a miserable garment!"

Akakii Akakievich's heart sank at these words.

"Why is it impossible, Petrovich?" he said, almost in the pleading voice of a child: "all that ails it is, that it is worn on the shoulders. You must have some pieces." . . .

"Yes, patches could be found, patches are easily found," said Petrovich, "but there's nothing to sew them to. The thing is completely rotten: if you touch a needle to it—see, it will give way."

"Let it give way, and you can put on another patch at once."

"But there is nothing to put the patches on; there's no use in strengthening it; it is very far gone. It's lucky that it's cloth; for, if the wind were to blow, it would fly away."

"Well, strengthen it again. How this, in fact" . . .

"No," said Petrovich decisively, "there is nothing to be done with it. It's a thoroughly bad job. You'd better, when the cold winter weather comes on, make yourself some foot-bandages out of it, because stockings are not warm. The Germans invented them in order to make more money. [Petrovich loved, on occasion, to give a fling at the Germans.] But it is plain that you must have a new overcoat."

At the word *new*, all grew dark before Akakii Akakievich's eyes, and everything in the room began to whirl round. The only thing he saw clearly was the general with the paper face on Petrovich's snuff-box cover. "How a new one?" said he, as if still in a dream: "why, I have no money for that."

"Yes, a new one," said Petrovich, with barbarous composure.

"Well, if it came to a new one, how, it" . . .

"You mean how much would it cost?"

"Yes."

"Well, you would have to lay out a hundred and fifty or more," said Petrovich, and pursed up his lips significantly. He greatly liked powerful effects, liked to stun utterly and suddenly, and then to glance sideways to see what face the stunned person would put on the matter.

"A hundred and fifty rubles for an overcoat!" shrieked poor Akakii Akakievich—shrieked perhaps for the first time in his life, for his voice had always been distinguished for its softness.

"Yes, sir," said Petrovich, "for any sort of an overcoat. If you have marten fur on the collar, or a silk-lined hood, it will mount up to two hundred."

"Petrovich, please," said Akakii Akakievich in a beseeching tone, not hearing, and not trying to hear, Petrovich's words, and all his "effects," "some repairs, in order that it may wear yet a little longer."

"No, then, it would be a waste of labor and money," said Petrovich; and Akakii Akakievich went away after these words, utterly discouraged. But Petrovich stood long after his departure, with significantly compressed lips, and not betaking himself to his work, satisfied that he would not be dropped, and an artistic tailor employed.

Akakii Akakievich went out into the street as if in a dream. "Such an affair!" he said to himself: "I did not think it had come to" . . . and then after a pause, he added, "Well, so it is! see what it has come to at last! and I never imagined that it was so!" Then followed a long silence, after which he exclaimed, "Well, so it is! see what already exactly, nothing unexpected that . . . it would be nothing . . . what a circumstance!" So saying, instead of going home, he went in exactly the opposite direction without himself suspecting it.

On the way, a chimney-sweep brought his dirty side up against him, and blackened his whole shoulder: a whole hatful of rubbish landed on him from the top of a house which was building. He observed it not; and afterwards, when he ran into a sentry, who, having planted his halberd beside him, was shaking some snuff from his box into his horny hand— only then did he recover himself a little, and that because the sentry said, "Why are you thrusting yourself into a man's very face? Haven't you the sidewalk?" This caused him to look about him, and turn towards home.

There only, he finally began to collect his thoughts, and to survey his position in its clear and actual light, and to argue with himself, not brokenly, but sensibly and frankly, as with a reasonable friend, with whom one can discuss very private and personal matters. "No," said Akakii Akakievich, "it is impossible to reason with Petrovich now: he is that . . . evidently, his wife has been beating him. I'd better go to him Sunday morning: after Saturday night he will be a little cross-eyed and sleepy, for he will have to get drunk, and his wife won't give him any money; and at such a time, a ten-kopek piece in his hand will—he will become more fit to reason with, and then the overcoat, and that." . . .

Thus argued Akakii Akakievich with himself, regained his courage, and waited until the first Sunday, when, seeing from afar that Petrovich's wife had gone out of the house, he went straight to him. Petrovich's eye was very much askew, in fact, after Saturday: his head drooped, and he was very sleepy; but for all that, as soon as he knew what the question was, it seemed as though Satan jogged his memory. "Impossible," said he: "please to order a new one." Thereupon Akakii Akakievich handed over the ten-kopek piece. "Thank you, sir; I will drink your good health," said Petrovich: "but as for the overcoat, don't trouble yourself about it; it is good for nothing. I will make you a new coat famously, so let us settle about it now."

Akakii Akakievich was still for mending it; but Petrovich would not hear of it, and said, "I shall certainly make you a new one, and please depend upon it that I shall do my best. It may even be, as the fashion goes, that the collar can be fastened by silver hooks under a flap."

Then Akakii Akakievich saw that it was impossible to get along without a new overcoat, and his spirit sank utterly. How, in fact, was it to be accomplished? Where was the money to come from? He might, to be sure, depend, in part, upon his present at Christmas; but that money had long been doled out and allotted beforehand. He must have some new trousers, and pay a debt of long standing to the shoemaker for putting new tops to his old boots, and he must order three shirts from the seamstress, and a couple of pieces of linen which it is impolite to mention in print— in a word, all his money must be spent; and even if the director should be so kind as to order forty-five rubles instead of forty, or even fifty, it would be a mere nothing, and a mere drop in the ocean towards the capital necessary for an overcoat: although he knew that Petrovich was wrong-headed enough to blurt out some outrageous price, Satan only knows what, so that his own wife could not refrain from exclaiming, "Have you lost your senses, you fool?"

At one time he would not work at any price, and now it was quite likely that he had asked a price which it was not worth. Although he knew that Petrovich would undertake to make it for eighty rubles, still, where was he to get the eighty rubles? He might possibly manage half; yes, a half of that might be procured: but where was the other half to come from? But the reader must first be told where the first half came from. Akakii Akakievich had a habit of putting, for every ruble he spent, a groschen into a small box, fastened with lock and key, and with a hole in the top for the reception of money. At the end of each half-year, he counted over the heap of coppers, and changed it into small silver coins. This he continued for a long time; and thus, in the course of some years, the sum proved to amount to over forty rubles.

Thus he had one half on hand; but where to get the other half? where to get another forty rubles? Akakii Akakievich thought and thought, and decided that it would be necessary to curtail his ordinary expenses, for the space of one year at least—to dispense with tea in the evening; to burn no candles, and, if there was anything which he must do, to go into his landlady's room, and work by her light; when he went into the street, he must walk as lightly as possible, and as cautiously, upon the stones and flagging, almost upon tiptoe, in order not to wear out his heels in too short a time; he must give the laundress as little to wash as possible; and, in order not to wear out his clothes, he must take them off as soon as he got home, and wear only his cotton dressing-gown, which had been long and carefully saved.

To tell the truth, it was a little hard for him at first to accustom himself to these deprivations; but he got used to them at length, after a fashion, and all went smoothly—he even got used to being hungry in the evening; but he made up for it by treating himself in spirit, bearing ever in mind the thought of his future coat. From that time forth, his existence seemed to become, in some way, fuller, as if he were married, as if some other man lived in him, as if he were not alone, and some charming friend had consented to go along life's path with him—and the friend was no other than that overcoat, with thick wadding and a strong lining incapable of wearing out. He became more lively, and his character even became firmer, like that of a man who has made up his mind, and set himself a goal. From his face and gait, doubt and indecision—in short, all hesitating and wavering traits—disappeared of themselves.

Fire gleamed in his eyes: occasionally, the boldest and most daring ideas flitted through his mind; why not, in fact, have marten fur on the collar? The thought of this nearly made him absent-minded. Once, in copying a letter, he nearly made a mistake, so that he exclaimed almost aloud, "Ugh!" and crossed himself. Once in the course of each month, he had a conference with Petrovich on the subject of the coat—where it would be better to buy the cloth, and the color, and the price—and he always returned home satisfied, though troubled, reflecting that the time would come at last when it could all be bought, and then the overcoat could be made.

The matter progressed more briskly than he had expected. Far beyond all his hopes, the director appointed neither forty nor forty-five rubles for Akakii Akakievich's share, but sixty. Did he suspect that Akakii Akakievich needed an overcoat? or did it merely happen so? at all events, twenty extra rubles were by this means provided. This circumstance hastened matters. Only two or three months more of hunger—and Akakii Akakievich had accumulated about eighty rubles. His heart, generally so quiet, began to beat.

On the first possible day, he visited the shops in company with Petrovich. They purchased some very good cloth—and reasonably, for they had been considering the matter for six months, and rarely did a month pass without their visiting the shops to inquire prices; and Petrovich said himself, that no better cloth could be had. For lining, they selected a cotton stuff, but so firm and thick, that Petrovich declared it to be better than silk, and even prettier and more glossy. They did not buy the marten fur, because it was dear, in fact; but in its stead, they picked out the very best of cat-skin which could be found in the shop, and which might be taken for marten at a distance.

Petrovich worked at the coat two whole weeks, for there was a great deal of quilting: otherwise it would have been done sooner. Petrovich charged twelve rubles for his work—it could not possibly be done for less: it was all sewed with silk, in small, double seams; and Petrovich went over each seam afterwards with his own teeth, stamping in various patterns.

It was—it is difficult to say precisely on what day, but it was probably the most glorious day in Akakii Akakievich's life, when Petrovich at length brought home the coat. He brought it in the morning, before the hour when it was necessary to go to the department. Never did a coat arrive so exactly in the nick of time; for the severe cold had set in, and it seemed to threaten increase. Petrovich presented himself with the coat as befits a good tailor. On his countenance was a significant expression, such as Akakii Akakievich had never beheld there. He seemed sensible to the fullest extent that he had done no small deed, and that a gulf had suddenly appeared, separating tailors who only put in linings, and make repairs, from those who make new things.

He took the coat out of the large pocket-handkerchief in which he had brought it. (The handkerchief was fresh from the laundress: he now removed it, and put it in his pocket for use.) Taking out the coat, he gazed proudly at it, held it with both hands, and flung it very skilfully over the shoulders of Akakii Akakievich; then he pulled it and fitted it down behind with his hand; then he draped it around Akakii Akakievich without buttoning it. Akakii Akakievich, as a man advanced in life, wished to try the sleeves. Petrovich helped him on with them, and it turned out that the sleeves were satisfactory also. In short, the coat appeared to be perfect, and just in season.

Petrovich did not neglect this opportunity to observe that it was only because he lived in a narrow street, and had no signboard, and because he had known Akakii Akakievich so long, that he had made it so cheaply; but, if he had been on the Nevsky Prospect, he would have charged seventy-five rubles for the making alone. Akakii Akakievich did not care to argue this point with Petrovich, and he was afraid of the large sums with which Petrovich was fond of raising the dust. He paid him, thanked him, and set out at once in his new coat for the department. Petrovich followed him, and, pausing in the street, gazed long at the coat in the distance, and went to one side expressly to run through a crooked alley, and emerge again into the street to gaze once more upon the coat from another point, namely, directly in front.

Meantime Akakii Akakievich went on with every sense in holiday mood. He was conscious every second of the time, that he had a new overcoat on his shoulders; and several times he laughed with internal satisfaction. In fact, there were two advantages—one was its warmth; the other, its beauty. He saw nothing of the road, and suddenly found himself at the department. He threw off his coat in the ante-room, looked it over well, and confided it to the especial care of the janitor. It is impossible to say just how every one in the department knew at once that Akakii Akakievich had a new coat, and that the "mantle" no longer existed. All rushed at the same moment into the ante-room, to inspect Akakii Akakievich's new coat. They began to congratulate him, and to say pleasant things to him, so that he began at first to smile, and then he grew ashamed.

When all surrounded him, and began to say that the new coat must be "christened," and that he must give a whole evening at least to it, Akakii Akakievich lost his head completely, knew not where he stood, what to answer, and how to get out of it. He stood blushing all over for several minutes, and was on the point of assuring them with great simplicity that it was not a new coat, that it was so and so, that it was the old coat. At length one of the officials, some assistant chief probably, in order to show that he was not at all proud, and on good terms with his inferiors, said, "So be it: I will give the party instead of Akakii Akakievich; I invite you all to tea with me to-night; it happens quite *apropos*, as it is my name-day."

The officials naturally at once offered the assistant chief their congratulations, and accepted the invitation with pleasure. Akakii Akakievich would have declined; but all declared that it was discourteous, that it was simply a sin and a shame, and that he could not possibly refuse. Besides, the idea became pleasant to him when he recollected that he should thereby have a chance to wear his new coat in the evening also.

That whole day was truly a most triumphant festival day for Akakii Akakievich. He returned home in the most happy frame of mind, threw off his coat, and hung it carefully on the wall, admiring afresh the cloth and the lining; and then he brought out his old, worn-out coat, for comparison. He looked at it, and laughed, so vast was the difference. And long after dinner he laughed again when the condition of the "mantle" recurred to his mind. He dined gayly, and after dinner wrote nothing, no papers even, but took his ease for a while on the bed, until it got dark. Then he dressed himself leisurely, put on his coat, and stepped out into the street.

Where the host lived, unfortunately we cannot say: our memory begins to fail us badly; and everything in St. Petersburg, all the houses and streets, have run together, and become so mixed up in our head, that it is very difficult to produce anything thence in proper form. At all events, this much is certain, that the official lived in the best part of the city; and therefore it must have been anything but near to Akakii Akakievich.

Akakii Akakievich was first obliged to traverse a sort of wilderness of deserted, dimly lighted streets; but in proportion as he approached the official's quarter of the city, the streets became more lively, more populous, and more brilliantly illuminated. Pedestrians began to appear; handsomely dressed ladies were more frequently encountered; the men had otter collars; peasant wagoners, with their grate-like sledges stuck full of gilt nails, became rarer; on the other hand, more and more coachmen in red velvet caps, with lacquered sleighs and bear-skin robes, began to appear; carriages with decorated coach-boxes flew swiftly through the streets, their wheels scrunching the snow.

Akakii Akakievich gazed upon all this as upon a novelty. He had not been in the streets during the evening for years. He halted out of curiosity before the lighted window of a shop, to look at a picture representing a handsome woman, who had thrown off her shoe, thereby baring her whole foot in a very pretty way; and behind her the head of a man with side-whiskers and a handsome mustache peeped from the door of another room. Akakii Akakievich shook his head, and laughed, and then went on his way. Why did he laugh? Because he had met with a thing utterly unknown, but for which every one cherishes, nevertheless, some sort of feeling; or else he thought, like many officials, as follows: "Well, those French! What is to be said? If they like anything of that sort, then, in fact, that" . . . But possibly he did not think that. For it is impossible to enter a man's mind, and know all that he thinks.

At length he reached the house in which the assistant chief lodged. The assistant chief lived in fine style: on the staircase burned a lantern; his apartment was on the second floor. On entering the vestibule, Akakii Akakievich beheld a whole row of overshoes on the floor. Amid them, in the centre of the room, stood a samovar, humming, and emitting clouds of steam. On the walls hung all sorts of coats and cloaks, among which there were even some with beaver collars or velvet facings. Beyond the wall the buzz of conversation was audible, which became clear and loud when the servant came out with a trayful of empty glasses, cream-jugs, and sugar-bowls. It was evident that the officials had arrived long before, and had already finished their first glass of tea.

Akakii Akakievich, having hung up his own coat, entered the room; and before him all at once appeared lights, officials, pipes, card-tables; and he was surprised by a sound of rapid conversation rising from all the tables, and the noise of moving chairs. He halted very awkwardly in the middle of the room, wondering, and trying to decide, what he ought to do. But they had seen him: they received him with a shout, and all went out at once into the ante-room, and took another look at his coat. Akakii Akakievich, although somewhat confused, was open-hearted, and could not refrain from rejoicing when he saw how they praised his coat. Then, of course, they all dropped him and his coat, and returned, as was proper, to the tables set out for whist. All this—the noise, talk, and throng of people—was rather wonderful to Akakii Akakievich. He simply did not know where he stood, or where to put his hands, his feet, and his whole body. Finally he sat down by the players, looked at the cards, gazed at the face of one and another, and after a while began to gape, and to feel that it was wearisome—the more so, as the hour was already long past when he usually went to bed. He wanted to take leave of the host; but they would not let him go, saying that he must drink a glass of champagne, in honor of his new garment, without fail.

In the course of an hour, supper was served, consisting of vegetable salad, cold veal, pastry, confectioner's pies, and champagne. They made Akakii Akakievich drink two glasses of champagne, after which he felt that the room grew livelier: still, he could not forget that it was twelve o'clock, and that he should have been at home long ago. In order that the host might not think of some excuse for detaining him, he went out of the room quietly, sought out, in the ante-room, his overcoat, which, to his sorrow, he found lying on the floor, brushed it, picked off every speck, put it on his shoulders, and descended the stairs to the street.

In the street all was still bright. Some petty shops, those permanent clubs of servants and all sorts of people, were open: others were shut, but, nevertheless, showed a streak of light the whole length of the door-crack, indicating that they were not yet free of company, and that probably domestics, both male and female, were finishing their stories and conversations, leaving their masters in complete ignorance as to their whereabouts.

Akakii Akakievich went on in a happy frame of mind: he even started to run, without knowing why, after some lady, who flew past like a flash of lightning, and whose whole body was endowed with an extraordinary amount of movement. But he stopped short, and went on very quietly as before, wondering whence he had got that gait. Soon there spread before him those deserted streets, which are not cheerful in the daytime, not to mention the evening. Now they were even more dim and lonely: the lanterns began to grow rarer—oil, evidently, had been less liberally supplied; then came wooden houses and fences: not a soul anywhere; only the snow sparkled in the streets, and mournfully darkled the low-roofed cabins with their closed shutters. He approached the place where the street crossed an endless square with barely visible houses on its farther side, and which seemed a fearful desert.

Afar, God knows where, a tiny spark glimmered from some sentry-box, which seemed to stand on the edge of the world. Akakii Akakievich's cheerfulness diminished at this point in a marked degree. He entered the square, not without an involuntary sensation of fear, as though his heart warned him of some evil. He glanced back and on both sides—it was like a sea about him. "No, it is better not to look," he thought, and went on, closing his eyes; and when he opened them, to see whether he was near the end of the square, he suddenly beheld, standing just before his very nose, some bearded individuals—of just what sort, he could not make out. All grew dark before his eyes, and his breast throbbed.

"But of course the coat is mine!" said one of them in a loud voice, seizing hold of the collar. Akakii Akakievich was about to shout for the watch, when the second man thrust a fist into his mouth, about the size of an official's head, muttering, "Now scream!"

Akakii Akakievich felt them take off his coat, and give him a push with a knee: he fell headlong upon the snow, and felt no more. In a few minutes he recovered consciousness, and rose to his feet; but no one was there. He felt that it was cold in the square, and that his coat was gone: he began to shout, but his voice did not appear to reach to the outskirts of the square. In despair, but without ceasing to shout, he started on a run through the square, straight towards the sentry-box, beside which stood the watchman, leaning on his halberd, and apparently curious to know what devil of a man was running towards him from afar, and shouting. Akakii Akakievich ran up to him, and began in a sobbing voice to shout that he was asleep, and attended to nothing, and did not see when a man was robbed. The watchman replied that he had seen no one; that he had seen two men stop him in the middle of the square, and supposed that they were friends of his; and that, instead of scolding in vain, he had better go to the captain on the morrow, so that the captain might investigate as to who had stolen the coat.

Akakii Akakievich ran home in complete disorder: his hair, which grew very thinly upon his temples and the back of his head, was entirely disarranged; his side and breast, and all his trousers, were covered with snow. The old woman, mistress of his lodgings, hearing a terrible knocking, sprang hastily from her bed, and, with a shoe on one foot only, ran to open the door, pressing the sleeve of her chemise to her bosom out of modesty; but when she had opened it, she fell back on beholding Akakii Akakievich in such a state.

When he told the matter, she clasped her hands, and said that he must go straight to the superintendent, for the captain would turn up his nose, promise well, and drop the matter there: the very best thing to do, would be to go to the superintendent; that he knew her, because Finnish Anna, her former cook, was now nurse at the superintendent's; that she often saw him passing the house; and that he was at church every Sunday, praying, but at the same time gazing cheerfully at everybody; and that he must be a good man, judging from all appearances.

Having listened to this opinion, Akakii Akakievich betook himself sadly to his chamber; and how he spent the night there, any one can imagine who can put himself in another's place. Early in the morning, he presented himself at the superintendent's, but they told him that he was asleep. He went again at ten—and was again informed that he was asleep. He went at eleven o'clock, and they said, "The superintendent is not at home." At dinner-time, the clerks in the ante-room would not admit him on any terms, and insisted upon knowing his business, and what brought him, and how it had come about—so that at last, for once in his life, Akakii Akakievich felt an inclination to show some spirit, and said curtly that he must see the superintendent in person; that they should not presume to refuse him entrance; that he came from the department of justice, and, when he complained of them, they would see.

The clerks dared make no reply to this, and one of them went to call the superintendent. The superintendent listened to the extremely strange story of the theft of the coat. Instead of directing his attention to the principal points of the matter, he began to question Akakii Akakievich. Why did he return so late? Was he in the habit of going, or had he been, to any disorderly house? So that Akakii Akakievich got thoroughly confused, and left him without knowing whether the affair of his overcoat was in proper train, or not.

All that day he never went near the court (for the first time in his life). The next day he made his appearance, very pale, and in his old "mantle," which had become even more shabby. The news of the robbery of the coat touched many; although there were officials present who never omitted an opportunity, even the present, to ridicule Akakii Akakievich. They decided to take up a collection for him on the spot, but it turned out a mere trifle; for the officials had already spent a great deal in subscribing for the director's portrait, and for some book, at the suggestion of the head of that division, who was a friend of the author: and so the sum was trifling.

One, moved by pity, resolved to help Akakii Akakievich with some good advice at least, and told him that he ought not to go to the captain, for although it might happen that the police-captain, wishing to win the approval of his superior officers, might hunt up the coat by some means, still, the coat would remain in the possession of the police if he did not offer legal proof that it belonged to him: the best thing for him would be to apply to a certain *prominent personage*; that this *prominent personage*, by entering into relations with the proper persons, could greatly expedite the matter.

As there was nothing else to be done, Akakii Akakievich decided to go to the *prominent personage*. What was the official position of the *prominent personage*, remains unknown to this day. The reader must know that the *prominent personage* had but recently become a prominent personage, but up to that time he had been an insignificant person.

Moreover, his present position was not considered prominent in comparison with others more prominent. But there is always a circle of people to whom what is insignificant in the eyes of others, is always important enough. Moreover, he strove to increase his importance by many devices; namely, he managed to have the inferior officials meet him on the staircase when he entered upon his service: no one was to presume to come directly to him, but the strictest etiquette must be observed; the "Collegiate Recorder" must announce to the government secretary, the government secretary to the titular councillor, or whatever other man was proper, and the business came before him in this manner. In holy Russia, all is thus contaminated with the love of imitation: each man imitates and copies his superior. They even say that a certain titular councillor, when promoted to the head of some little separate courtroom, immediately partitioned off a private room for himself, called it the *Audience Chamber*, and posted at the door a lackey with red collar and braid, who grasped the handle of the door, and opened to all comers; though the audience chamber would hardly hold an ordinary writing-table.

The manners and customs of the *prominent personage* were grand and imposing, but rather exaggerated. The main foundation of his system was strictness. "Strictness, strictness, and always strictness!" he generally said; and at the last word he looked significantly into the face of the person to whom he spoke. But there was no necessity for this, for the half-score of officials who formed the entire force of the mechanism of the office were properly afraid without it: on catching sight of him afar off, they left their work, and waited, drawn up in line, until their chief had passed through the room. His ordinary converse with his inferiors smacked of sternness, and consisted chiefly of three phrases: "How dare you?" "Do you know to whom you are talking?" "Do you realize who stands before you?"

Otherwise he was a very kind-hearted man, good to his comrades, and ready to oblige; but the rank of general threw him completely off his balance. On receiving that rank, he became confused, as it were, lost his way, and never knew what to do. If he chanced to be with his equals, he was still a very nice kind of man—a very good fellow in many respects, and not stupid: but just the moment that he happened to be in the society of people but one rank lower than himself, he was simply incomprehensible; he became silent; and his situation aroused sympathy, the more so, as he felt himself that he might have made an incomparably better use of the time. In his eyes, there was sometimes visible a desire to join some interesting conversation and circle; but he was held back by the thought, Would it not be a very great condescension on his part? Would it not be familiar? and would he not thereby lose his importance? And in consequence of such reflections, he remained ever in the same dumb state, uttering only occasionally a few monosyllabic sounds, and thereby earning the name of the most tiresome of men.

To this *prominent personage*, our Akakii Akakievich presented himself, and that at the most unfavorable time, very inopportune for himself, though opportune for the *prominent personage*. The prominent personage was in his cabinet, conversing very, very gayly with a recently arrived old acquaintance and companion of his childhood, whom he had not seen for several years. At such a time it was announced to him that a person named Bashmachkin had come. He asked abruptly, "Who is he?" "Some official," they told him. "Ah, he can wait! this is no time," said the important man. It must be remarked here, that the important man lied outrageously: he had said all he had to say to his friend long before; and the conversation had been interspersed for some time with very long pauses, during which they merely slapped each other on the leg, and said, "You think so, Ivan Abramovich!" "Just so, Stepan Varlamovich!" Nevertheless, he ordered that the official should wait, in order to show his friend—a man who had not been in the service for a long time, but had lived at home in the country—how long officials had to wait in his ante-room.

At length, having talked himself completely out, and more than that, having had his fill of pauses, and smoked a cigar in a very comfortable arm-chair with reclining back, he suddenly seemed to recollect, and told the secretary, who stood by the door with papers of reports, "Yes, it seems, indeed, that there is an official standing there. Tell him that he may come in." On perceiving Akakii Akakievich's modest mien, and his worn undress uniform, he turned abruptly to him, and said, "What do you want?" in a curt, hard voice, which he had practised in his room in private, and before the looking-glass, for a whole week before receiving his present rank.

Akakii Akakievich, who already felt betimes the proper amount of fear, became somewhat confused: and as well as he could, as well as his tongue would permit, he explained, with a rather more frequent addition than usual of the word *that*, that his overcoat was quite new, and had been stolen in the most inhuman manner; that he had applied to him, in order that he might, in some way, by his intermediation, that . . . he might enter into correspondence with the chief superintendent of police, and find the coat.

For some inexplicable reason, this conduct seemed familiar to the general. "What, my dear sir!" he said abruptly, "don't you know etiquette? Where have you come to? Don't you know how matters are managed? You should first have entered a complaint about this at the court: it would have gone to the head of the department, to the chief of the division, then it would have been handed over to the secretary, and the secretary would have given it to me." . . .

"But, your excellency," said Akakii Akakievich, trying to collect his small handful of wits, and conscious at the same time that he was perspiring terribly, "I, your excellency, presumed to trouble you because secretaries that . . . are an untrustworthy race." . . .

"What, what, what!" said the *important personage*. "Where did you get such courage? Where did you get such ideas? What impudence towards their chiefs and superiors has spread among the young generation!" The prominent personage apparently had not observed that Akakii Akakievich was already in the neighborhood of fifty. If he could be called a young man, then it must have been in comparison with some one who was seventy. "Do you know to whom you speak? Do you realize who stands before you? Do you realize it? do you realize it? I ask you!" Then he stamped his foot, and raised his voice to such a pitch that it would have frightened even a different man from Akakii Akakievich.

Akakii Akakievich's senses failed him; he staggered, trembled in every limb, and could not stand; if the porters had not run in to support him, he would have fallen to the floor. They carried him out insensible. But the prominent personage, gratified that the effect should have surpassed his expectations, and quite intoxicated with the thought that his word could even deprive a man of his senses, glanced sideways at his friend in order to see how he looked upon this, and perceived, not without satisfaction, that his friend was in a most undecided frame of mind, and even beginning, on his side, to feel a trifle frightened.

Akakii Akakievich could not remember how he descended the stairs, and stepped into the street. He felt neither his hands nor feet. Never in his life had he been so rated by any general, let alone a strange one. He went on through the snow-storm, which was howling through the streets, with his mouth wide open, slipping off the sidewalk: the wind, in Petersburg fashion, flew upon him from all quarters, and through every cross-street. In a twinkling it had blown a quinsy into his throat, and he reached home unable to utter a word: his throat was all swollen, and he lay down on his bed. So powerful is sometimes a good scolding!

The next day a violent fever made its appearance. Thanks to the generous assistance of the Petersburg climate, his malady progressed more rapidly than could have been expected: and when the doctor arrived, he found, on feeling his pulse, that there was nothing to be done, except to prescribe a fomentation, merely that the sick man might not be left without the beneficent aid of medicine; but at the same time, he predicted his end in another thirty-six hours. After this, he turned to the landlady, and said, "And as for you, my dear, don't waste your time on him: order his pine coffin now, for an oak one will be too expensive for him."

Did Akakii Akakievich hear these fatal words? and, if he heard them, did they produce any overwhelming effect upon him? Did he lament the bitterness of his life?—We know not, for he continued in a raving, parching condition. Visions incessantly appeared to him, each stranger than the other: now he saw Petrovich, and ordered him to make a coat, with some traps for robbers, who seemed to him to be always under the bed; and he cried, every moment, to the landlady to pull one robber from under his coverlet: then he inquired why his old "mantle" hung before him when he had a new overcoat; then he fancied that he was standing before the general, listening to a thorough setting-down, and saying, "Forgive, your excellency!" but at last he began to curse, uttering the most horrible words, so that his aged landlady crossed herself, never in her life having heard anything of the kind from him—the more so, as those words followed directly after the words *your excellency*. Later he talked utter nonsense, of which nothing could be understood: all that was evident, was that his incoherent words and thoughts hovered ever about one thing—his coat.

At last poor Akakii Akakievich breathed his last. They sealed up neither his room nor his effects, because, in the first place, there were no heirs, and, in the second, there was very little inheritance; namely, a bunch of goose-quills, a quire of white official paper, three pairs of socks, two or three buttons which had burst off his trousers, and the "mantle" already known to the reader. To whom all this fell, God knows. I confess that the person who told this tale took no interest in the matter. They carried Akakii Akakievich out, and buried him. And Petersburg was left without Akakii Akakievich, as though he had never lived there. A being disappeared, and was hidden, who was protected by none, dear to none, interesting to none, who never even attracted to himself the attention of an observer of nature, who omits no opportunity of thrusting a pin through a common fly, and examining it under the microscope—a being who bore meekly the jibes of the department, and went to his grave without having done one unusual deed, but to whom, nevertheless, at the close of his life, appeared a bright visitant in the form of a coat, which momentarily cheered his poor life, and upon whom, thereafter, an intolerable misfortune descended, just as it descends upon the heads of the mighty of this world! . . .

Several days after his death, the porter was sent from the department to his lodgings, with an order for him to present himself immediately ("The chief commands it!"). But the porter had to return unsuccessful, with the answer that he could not come; and to the question, Why? he explained in the words, "Well, because: he is already dead! he was buried four days ago." In this manner did they hear of Akakii Akakievich's death at the department; and the next day a new and much larger official sat in his place, forming his letters by no means upright, but more inclined and slantwise.

But who could have imagined that this was not the end of Akakii Akakievich—that he was destined to raise a commotion after death, as if in compensation for his utterly insignificant life? But so it happened, and our poor story unexpectedly gains a fantastic ending.

A rumor suddenly spread throughout Petersburg that a dead man had taken to appearing on the Kalinkin Bridge, and far beyond, at night, in the form of an official seeking a stolen coat, and that, under the pretext of its being the stolen coat, he dragged every one's coat from his shoulders without regard to rank or calling—cat-skin, beaver, wadded, fox, bear, raccoon coats; in a word, every sort of fur and skin which men adopted for their covering. One of the department employés saw the dead man with his own eyes, and immediately recognized in him Akakii Akakievich: nevertheless, this inspired him with such terror, that he started to run with all his might, and therefore could not examine thoroughly, and only saw how the latter threatened him from afar with his finger.

Constant complaints poured in from all quarters, that the backs and shoulders, not only of titular but even of court councillors, were entirely exposed to the danger of a cold, on account of the frequent dragging off of their coats. Arrangements were made by the police to catch the corpse, at any cost, alive or dead, and punish him as an example to others, in the most severe manner: and in this they nearly succeeded; for a policeman, on guard in Kirushkin Alley, caught the corpse by the collar on the very scene of his evil deeds, for attempting to pull off the frieze coat of some retired musician who had blown the flute in his day.

Having seized him by the collar, he summoned, with a shout, two of his comrades, whom he enjoined to hold him fast, while he himself felt for a moment in his boot, in order to draw thence his snuff-box, to refresh his six times forever frozen nose; but the snuff was of a sort which even a corpse could not endure. The policeman had no sooner succeeded, having closed his right nostril with his finger, in holding half a handful up to the left, than the corpse sneezed so violently that he completely filled the eyes of all three. While they raised their fists to wipe them, the dead man vanished utterly, so that they positively did not know whether they had actually had him in their hands at all. Thereafter the watchmen conceived such a terror of dead men, that they were afraid even to seize the living, and only screamed from a distance, "Hey, there! go your way!" and the dead official began to appear, even beyond the Kalinkin Bridge, causing no little terror to all timid people.

But we have totally neglected that *certain prominent personage*, who may really be considered as the cause of the fantastic turn taken by this true history. First of all, justice compels us to say, that after the departure of poor, thoroughly annihilated Akakii Akakievich, he felt something like remorse. Suffering was unpleasant to him: his heart was accessible to many good impulses, in spite of the fact that his rank very often prevented his showing his true self. As soon as his friend had left his cabinet, he began to think about poor Akakii Akakievich. And from that day forth, poor Akakii Akakievich, who could not bear up under an official reprimand, recurred to his mind almost every day. The thought of the latter troubled him to such an extent, that a week later he even resolved to send an official to him, to learn whether he really could assist him; and when it was reported to him that Akakii Akakievich had died suddenly of fever, he was startled, listened to the reproaches of his conscience, and was out of sorts for the whole day.

Wishing to divert his mind in some way, and forget the disagreeable impression, he set out that evening for one of his friends' houses, where he found quite a large party assembled; and, what was better, nearly every one was of the same rank, so that he need not feel in the least constrained. This had a marvellous effect upon his mental state. He expanded, made himself agreeable in conversation, charming: in short, he passed a delightful evening. After supper he drank a couple of glasses of champagne—not a bad recipe for cheerfulness, as every one knows. The champagne inclined him to various out-of-the-way adventures; and, in particular, he determined not to go home, but to go to see a certain well-known lady, Karolina Ivanovna, a lady, it appears, of German extraction, with whom he felt on a very friendly footing.

It must be mentioned that the prominent personage was no longer a young man, but a good husband, and respected father of a family. Two sons, one of whom was already in the service, and a good-looking, sixteen-year-old daughter, with a rather *retroussé* but pretty little nose, came every morning to kiss his hand, and say, "*Bonjour*, papa." His wife, a still fresh and good-looking woman, first gave him her hand to kiss, and then, reversing the procedure, kissed his. But the prominent personage, though perfectly satisfied in his domestic relations, considered it stylish to have a friend in another quarter of the city. This friend was hardly prettier or younger than his wife; but there are such puzzles in the world, and it is not our place to judge them.

So the important personage descended the stairs, stepped into his sleigh, and said to the coachman, "To Karolina Ivanovna's," and, wrapping himself luxuriously in his warm coat, found himself in that delightful position than which a Russian can conceive nothing better, which is, when you think of nothing yourself, yet the thoughts creep into your mind of their own accord, each more agreeable than the other, giving you no trouble to drive them away, or seek them. Fully satisfied, he slightly recalled all the gay points of the evening just passed, and all the *mots* which had made the small circle laugh. Many of them he repeated in a low voice, and found them quite as funny as before; and therefore it is not surprising that he should laugh heartily at them.

Occasionally, however, he was hindered by gusts of wind, which, coming suddenly, God knows whence or why, cut his face, flinging in it lumps of snow, filling out his coat-collar like a sail, or suddenly blowing it over his head with supernatural force, and thus causing him constant trouble to disentangle himself. Suddenly the important personage felt some one clutch him very firmly by the collar. Turning round, he perceived a man of short stature, in an old, worn uniform, and recognized, not without terror, Akakii Akakievich. The official's face was white as snow, and looked just like a corpse's. But the horror of the important personage transcended all bounds when he saw the dead man's mouth open, and, with a terrible odor of the grave, utter the following remarks:

"Ah, here you are at last! I have you, that . . . by the collar! I need your coat. You took no trouble about mine, but reprimanded me; now give up your own." The pallid prominent personage almost died. Brave as he was in the office and in the presence of inferiors generally, and although, at the sight of his manly form and appearance, every one said, "Ugh! how much character he has!" yet at this crisis, he, like many possessed of an heroic exterior, experienced such terror, that, not without cause, he began to fear an attack of illness.

He flung his coat hastily from his shoulders, and shouted to his coachman in an unnatural voice, "Home, at full speed!" The coachman, hearing the tone which is generally employed at critical moments, and even accompanied by something much more tangible, drew his head down between his shoulders in case of an emergency, flourished his knout, and flew on like an arrow. In a little more than six minutes the prominent personage was at the entrance of his own house.

Pale, thoroughly scared, and coatless, he went home instead of to Karolina Ivanovna's, got to his chamber after some fashion, and passed the night in the direst distress; so that the next morning over their tea, his daughter said plainly, "You are very pale to-day, papa." But papa remained silent, and said not a word to any one of what had happened to him, where he had been, or where he had intended to go.

This occurrence made a deep impression upon him. He even began to say less frequently to the under-officials, "How dare you? do you realize who stands before you?" and, if he did utter the words, it was after first having learned the bearings of the matter. But the most noteworthy point was, that from that day the apparition of the dead official quite ceased to be seen; evidently the general's overcoat just fitted his shoulders; at all events, no more instances of his dragging coats from people's shoulders were heard of.

But many active and apprehensive persons could by no means re-assure themselves, and asserted that the dead official still showed himself in distant parts of the city. And, in fact, one watchman in Kolomna saw with his own eyes the apparition come from behind a house; but being rather weak of body—so much so, that once upon a time an ordinary full-grown pig running out of a private house knocked him off his legs, to the great amusement of the surrounding public coachmen, from whom he demanded a groschen apiece for snuff, as damages—being weak, he dared not arrest him, but followed him in the dark, until, at length, the apparition looked round, paused, and inquired, "What do you want?" and showed such a fist as you never see on living men. The watchman said, "It's of no consequence," and turned back instantly. But the appari-tion was much too tall, wore huge mustaches, and, directing its steps apparently towards the Obukhoff Bridge, disappeared in the darkness of the night.

DOVER · THRIFT · EDITIONS

All books complete and unabridged. All 5³⁄₁₆″ × 8¼″, paperbound.
Just $1.00–$2.00 in U.S.A.

FICTION

THE MAN WHO WOULD BE KING AND OTHER STORIES, Rudyard Kipling. 128pp. 28051-9
$1.00

SELECTED SHORT STORIES, D. H. Lawrence. 128pp. 27794-1 $1.00

GREEN TEA AND OTHER GHOST STORIES, J. Sheridan LeFanu. 96pp. 27795-X $1.00

THE CALL OF THE WILD, Jack London. 64pp. 26472-6 $1.00

FIVE GREAT SHORT STORIES, Jack London. 96pp. 27063-7 $1.00

WHITE FANG, Jack London. 160pp. 26968-X $1.00

THE NECKLACE AND OTHER SHORT STORIES, Guy de Maupassant. 128pp. 27064-5 $1.00

BARTLEBY AND BENITO CERENO, Herman Melville. 112pp. 26473-4 $1.00

THE GOLD-BUG AND OTHER TALES, Edgar Allan Poe. 128pp. 26875-6 $1.00

THE QUEEN OF SPADES AND OTHER STORIES, Alexander Pushkin. 128pp. 28054-3 $1.00

THREE LIVES, Gertrude Stein. 176pp. 28059-4 $2.00

THE STRANGE CASE OF DR. JEKYLL AND MR. HYDE, Robert Louis Stevenson. 64pp.
26688-5 $1.00

TREASURE ISLAND, Robert Louis Stevenson. 160pp. 27559-0 $1.00

THE KREUTZER SONATA AND OTHER SHORT STORIES, Leo Tolstoy. 144pp. 27805-0 $1.00

ADVENTURES OF HUCKLEBERRY FINN, Mark Twain. 224pp. 28061-6 $2.00

THE MYSTERIOUS STRANGER AND OTHER STORIES, Mark Twain. 128pp. 27069-6 $1.00

CANDIDE, Voltaire (François-Marie Arouet). 112pp. 26689-3 $1.00

THE INVISIBLE MAN, H. G. Wells. 112pp. (Available in U.S. only.) 27071-8 $1.00

ETHAN FROME, Edith Wharton. 96pp. 26690-7 $1.00

THE PICTURE OF DORIAN GRAY, Oscar Wilde. 192pp. 27807-7 $1.00

NONFICTION

THE DEVIL'S DICTIONARY, Ambrose Bierce. 144pp. 27542-6 $1.00

THE SOULS OF BLACK FOLK, W. E. B. Du Bois. 176pp. 28041-1 $2.00

SELF-RELIANCE AND OTHER ESSAYS, Ralph Waldo Emerson. 128pp. 27790-9 $1.00

GREAT SPEECHES, Abraham Lincoln. 112pp. 26872-1 $1.00

THE PRINCE, Niccolò Machiavelli. 80pp. 27274-5 $1.00

SYMPOSIUM AND PHAEDRUS, Plato. 96pp. 27798-4 $1.00

THE TRIAL AND DEATH OF SOCRATES: FOUR DIALOGUES, Plato. 128pp. 27066-1 $1.00

CIVIL DISOBEDIENCE AND OTHER ESSAYS, Henry David Thoreau. 96pp. 27563-9 $1.00

THE THEORY OF THE LEISURE CLASS, Thorstein Veblen. 256pp. 28062-4 $2.00

PLAYS

THE CHERRY ORCHARD, Anton Chekhov. 64pp. 26682-6 $1.00

THE THREE SISTERS, Anton Chekhov. 64pp. 27544-2 $1.00

THE WAY OF THE WORLD, William Congreve. 80pp. 27787-9 $1.00

MEDEA, Euripides. 64pp. 27548-5 $1.00

THE MIKADO, William Schwenck Gilbert. 64pp. 27268-0 $1.00